# BROKEN LOVE

# BROKEN LOVE

*jillian dodd*

Jillian Dodd Inc.
N. Redington Beach, FL

ISBN: 978-1-946793-24-9
Second Edition

# dedication

This book is for my readers.

You inspire me every day with your kind words,
your loving hearts,
and your friendship.

# Books by Jillian Dodd

### The Keatyn Chronicles®
*Stalk Me*

*Kiss Me*

*Date Me*

*Love Me*

*Adore Me*

*Hate Me*

*Get Me*

### Hollywood Love Series
*Fame*

*Power*

*Money*

*Sex*

*Love*

### That Boy Series
*That Boy*

*That Wedding*

*That Baby*

### The Love Series
*Vegas Love*

*Broken Love*

### Spy Girl Series
*The Prince*

*The Eagle*

*The Society*

We're like two pieces split apart at birth who found their way back to each other. We're soul mates—a predestined pairing.

# Prologue
## Six Years Ago
### Cade

"YOU SON OF bitch!" Pike yells as he charges toward me then throws a punch at my face. "How could you do that?"

The blow knocks me back against the bar, and I fumble trying to steady myself. But I don't get time to recover. Pike slams his fist into my stomach. "I trusted you like a brother!"

"What the hell?" our friend Todd says, stepping between us and holding out his arms to keep the peace. "You're best friends. What's this all about?"

A livid Pike shoves Todd out of the way, knocking him to the ground. "What this is about is my best friend sleeping with my sister behind my back."

"I can explain," I say as his fist connects with my face again, this time cutting open my lip.

"There's nothing to explain, you cocksucker! You

fucked with my sister!"

"I wanted to tell you, Pike." I hold up my hands in an attempt to protect myself. "But she wouldn't let me!"

"That's a bullshit answer. We're best friends. Brothers. You betrayed me!"

He's right. I did.

"And then you broke her heart!" he yells furiously, slamming me with a fast barrage of punches that connect with my temple, ribs, stomach, jaw, and then nose.

I don't even try to stop him. I deserve this.

With the last punch, I spin in a circle and fall to the ground.

Pike glares down at me and spits on my shirt. "If you ever come near my sister again, I'll fucking kill you."

Then he turns and storms out of the bar.

The disgusted looks on our friends' faces rain down on me.

I lay on the bar floor and close my eyes, both my body and heart feeling completely broken.

# October 10th
## *Palmer*

"SO TELL ME all about your amazing travels," my friend and assistant, Tory, says. "I've only seen you for like five days in the last month." We are sipping martinis in the courtyard outside my home office, catching up.

"Going to Fashion Week is part of the job," I say with a shrug.

"Yeah, yeah. Must be rough. You're out gallivanting around—hitting New York, London, Milan, and Paris—while I'm back here holding down the fort."

"If I recall, you turned down my offer to accompany me. Something about a hot young stud?" I tease. Tory, who recently had her eleventh twenty-ninth birthday, is addicted to her personal trainer, Botox, and guys half her age.

"Sadly, that was over before your plane was wheels down in New York. It was for the best, though. He had a great body, but he couldn't carry an intelligent conversation. I had an epiphany while you were gone and realized that I'm attracted to more than just good looks."

"Does that mean you might consider dating guys who are out of college?"

She pours herself another drink, scoffing. "I've told you *many* times. Age is a state of mind. I've met some very mature twenty-year olds." She giggles. "Plus, at that age, they're so damn flirty. It turns me on. You should try dating someone *your* own age. You're still in your twenties. You're a beautiful actress. Why do you insist on dating older men?" She doesn't give me a chance to reply. "I know! I could set you up." She takes her phone out and scrolls through a list, landing on someone named *Scruff Boy*. "This is the guy I think you would like. He is so good-looking. Dark hair, gorgeous eyes, and the hottest scruff. He is so hot...he's pretty. Kind of like your former agent, Cade Crawford." She pauses and takes a drink.

"I survived another chance encounter with him when I was in New York City," I say, as I absentmindedly run my finger across the sugar rim and then lick it off.

"Palmer," she says with a dramatic sigh. "Do you ever think these 'chance encounters' aren't chance, but rather the universe putting two people together *over and over* until they finally smarten up and realize they were meant for each other?"

"Um, no. I don't think that."

"Fine," she huffs. "Tell me what happened."

"I walk into the VIP section of a club and the first

thing I see is Cade juggling a model on each knee, flirting and laughing. When he noticed me, the smile literally fell off his face."

"So what did you do? Just ignore him like usual?"

"I would have, but his brother, Carter—"

"Who you love. You love his whole family."

"I do." I nod in agreement. Cade has a wonderful, close-knit family.

"So what was Carter Crawford doing at Fashion Week? He's a sports agent. Shouldn't he have been at ESPN or something?"

I roll my eyes.

"Oh, duh," she says with a laugh. "*Models* are at Fashion Week, aren't they?"

I laugh and take another sip of my martini. "Uh, yeah. It's kind of their job. And you know those Crawford boys like to surround themselves with beautiful women."

"Like you?"

"It's been six years since Cade and I broke up. What is interesting, though, is that Carter looked to be pretty smitten with one particular model. Vale."

"Oh, Vale's really pretty."

"Aren't all models pretty?"

"Yeah," Tory concedes, "but Vale is different. She's not stick-thin like most. She's got big boobs like mine. And she was in that movie. I can't remember the name of it, but she was fucking funny. And she seems smart."

"Hey! I started out as a model. I'm not exactly dumb."

"Whatever," she says, refilling my glass. "You know what I'm saying."

"Well, if Vale's smart, she'll hang on to Carter. I swear, he just keeps getting hotter."

"You know you are really talking about Cade. All those boys look alike."

"I will admit that Cade looks good. Which pisses me off a little."

"I hate how men do that," she says. "They look sexier with crinkles around their eyes, a little grey at the temple."

"Ha!" I laugh. "How can you even say that? When was the last time you dated a guy your age?"

"Don't you curse at me," she says with a laugh. "Back to the club. What happened?"

"So, I said hi to Carter and gave him a hug. He introduced me to Vale. And Ashlyn Roberts was there, too."

"Oooh, has she read the script for the movie you're slated to be in? Is she interested in playing your sister?"

"She hadn't read it yet, but Cash had."

"Cash? He's the youngest Crawford brother, who has the twin sister, right?"

"Yep. I hadn't seen him in years. He went up north

for college and law school and is now back home working for Cade as a junior talent agent. Anyway, he said he really liked the script. Which is encouraging, because I think he and Ashlyn might have a little thing going on."

"Ohmigawd! I almost forgot!" Tory blurts out. "Did you hear what happened to Ashlyn? The whole sex tape thing?"

"Yeah, I felt so bad for her. I can't believe her asshole ex could do that. I hope she sues."

"That's old news, Palmer. I'm talking about her appearance on *The Elle Show*! When she was being interviewed, Elle told her that another sex tape had been released, and she started playing it."

"Oh my gosh! How horrible!"

"No, that's the thing. It wasn't. It was a video this guy did for her. Now I know why he looked so familiar. It was Cash Crawford. Anyway, I guess she and Cash met at a wedding, hooked up, then went to Vegas and got married! And then I'm not sure what happened, but they were like broken up. So in this video he was lying on the bed, shirtless. His hair was all messed up, and you can tell that he'd been fucking all night."

"How could you tell that?" I ask.

"I don't know. I just could. Stop interrupting me. Anyway, he was super sexy and muscular, and he had a dreamy voice, and he's all like, *I just married the most amazing girl last night.* And then he showed pictures of their night together. Taking selfies. A picture of her ass. Her asleep. And it was so damn cute. And Ashlyn was crying. And then someone from the audience yelled out, and she got up and was looking for him. And he was right there in the audience and then he proposed. And although you never saw them on screen, his whole family was there, I think—wait, you *have* to watch the video. It's gotten like a gazillion views. I can't believe you haven't seen it yet."

"I have been kind of busy," I tease. We watch as the video of *The Elle Show* plays—switching from Cash to Ashlyn's reactions. Then he proposes.

"It sounds like his whole family was there," I comment. "Oh, that's so sweet. She's really lucky."

"Do you want his family to do that for you?" she asks slyly.

"That will never happen, Tory."

"Come on, tell me for once what the deal is. Why did you really break up with that fine piece of man candy, and why can't you get back together?"

"We can't get back together because my brother, Pike, hates him."

"But why?"

"Pike and Cade were best friends. When we broke up, they got into a fist fight over it and haven't been friends since."

"And what about this?" she asks, pulling an envelope out of her pocket—the one I've been ignoring since I got home.

"It's probably just an invitation to another party I don't have the time to go to," I suggest, hoping she will leave it be.

"Why haven't you opened it yet?" she asks, turning it over and studying it.

"I just got home. I've been busy."

"I understand that. But what I want to know is why it didn't get put in my mail pile? I always reply to your invitations. It's, like, my job." She squints her eyes at me. "Oh, I see what this is. You were trying to hide it from me, weren't you? It's from the Crawford family in Laguna Hills. That's why you haven't opened it. Admit it."

"What if Cade is getting married?" My hand automatically goes to my chest. I'm not sure my heart could take it if he did. No matter how much I pretend to hate him.

"Well, let's take a look." She rips it open. "It says here that Cash Crawford and Ashlyn Roberts are getting married—tomorrow. You're invited, and you're going to attend."

"No, I'm not. I can't."

"I'll be your plus one," she says sweetly as she refills my martini from the pitcher we made earlier. "That way I know you can't back out."

# October 11th
## *Cade*

"CAN YOU BELIEVE our little brother is actually getting married?" I whisper to my other younger brother, Carter. We're dressed in tuxedos, lined up at the altar, and ready for the wedding processional.

"He looks nervous," Carter says. "Don't you think so, Cade?"

Cash shushes us. "I'm not nervous. I'm just excited to see Ashlyn in her wedding dress."

"And can't wait for the honeymoon, I bet," Carter teases, elbowing him.

I start to say something in reply, but my voice catches in my throat as my heart skips a beat.

Palmer Montlake is being escorted down the aisle by an usher.

And she looks beautiful.

Like I pictured she would have on our wedding day.

Her blonde hair is done up, and little wispy tendrils frame her face. Her long dress is blowing in the ocean breeze. Palmer was my first real love. My only real love.

Which was crazy. We're complete opposites. She's six years younger than me. But she's amazing—free-spirited, stubborn, tenacious, and beautiful. She used to squeeze the toothpaste from the middle. Drove me nuts, but I was so enamored with her that I didn't care.

For a brief, wonderful moment, I imagine her walking toward me, getting ready to marry me, like she should have all those years ago.

When she takes a seat, I stop holding my breath, letting it out with a whoosh.

The good news is she's with her friend, Tory, and not with some guy—or worse, her brother. I would have kicked Cash's ass, special day or not, if he would have invited Pike Montlake to his wedding.

I pry my attention away from Palmer as my parents start the wedding processional.

We're in a wood-beamed, stained glass chapel perched at the top of a cliff, overlooking the ocean. Cash told me that when he and Ashlyn were visiting wedding locations, this one stood out right away because it reminded them of their—not legally binding—Vegas wedding. Palmer and I weren't engaged long enough to plan our wedding. It was a weekend of bliss, followed by the fight that ruined everything.

My little sister, Cash's twin, is Ashlyn's maid of honor. She looks shockingly different than she did at the rehearsal dinner last night—where her hair was black with blue streaks. Chloe is an artistic jewelry designer who changes her hair almost as often as she does her underwear. Tonight she looks almost demure in her natural brown color, but black motorcycle boots peek out from under her bridesmaid gown, and when she gets up to the altar, she puts her hand in front of her chest so no one behind her can see and then, in true Chloe form, she flips us all the bird.

We're chuckling until "Here Comes The Bride" starts playing, and Ashlyn makes her way down the aisle.

Ashlyn's eyes sparkle with joy and, although my brother is beaming from ear to ear, he's choked up.

I feel emotional, too.

My baby bro is getting married.

And the love of my life is here to see it.

# *Palmer*

WHEN I WALK down the aisle to take my seat, I can't help but notice Cade standing at the altar with his brothers. His unruly dirty blonde hair is slicked back neatly and his usual scruffy face is clean-shaven, revealing a strong jawline and lush lips designed for pleasure.

I'm fantasizing about all the things those lips used to do to me, when Tory leans over and says, "You do realize this is your dream wedding?"

"No, it's not. I wouldn't want anything so elaborate."

"Remember the night we got drunk on homemade sangria and binge watched wedding shows?"

"Barely," I whisper, rolling my eyes at her. "Obviously, I didn't know what the hell I was saying."

"Every girl dreams of a wedding like this, don't you think? Princess ball gown, handsome groom, gorgeous flowers, beautiful location, and everyone you know here to watch."

I shush her as the ceremony begins.

MY HEART SURVIVES the trauma of seeing a tuxedo-clad Cade standing at the end of the aisle in front of me, and before I know it, the ceremony is over and we're grabbing champagne off a platter on a brick patio surrounded by candles flickering in hurricane lanterns.

It takes me back.

*Cade and I in a helicopter, flying over the snowy mountains. And, there, set on a perfect flat peak, is a ring of flickering lanterns.*

*"Cade, look at how pretty and romantic that is."*

*"Yeah, cool," he says, seemingly unimpressed as we pass by.*

*A few minutes later, we land at a lodge, where we are greeted by an elderly man and his wife, suited up in ski coveralls, and then offered a snowmobile.*

*We take off up the snow-covered slope, my arms wrapped tightly around Cade as he drives. The scenery is gorgeous. The thick pine trees smell of the impending holiday season, and powdery snow shimmers in the moonlight.*

*We wind our way to the top of the mountain and then stop—at the ring of lanterns that I saw from above. Only now, I can see a table for two set inside the ring.*

*"Cade, what is all this?" I ask.*

*"All this is our first date."*

"Admit it," Tory says, clinking my champagne flute with hers and bringing me back to the present. "You've still got a thing for him."

"Don't be silly. It was a long time ago."

"Based on the way you were eye-fucking the shit out of him, I'd say time doesn't matter."

"I was not! I shouldn't be here. It's all my fault Cade and I broke up. I should have apologized to him a long time ago."

"Maybe you should do that tonight. In the meantime, I've got my eye on groomsman number three. Do you know who he is?"

"Friend of the groom," I say with a sly smile.

"Yes, *that* was in the wedding program. Which is slightly bothersome as it probably means they went to college together, and I'm going to have to go cougar. *Again.* Don't care, though. He's hot. And I didn't see a ring. Come on, let's do a drive by."

"A drive by?"

"Yes, we're casually going to walk to that bar over there, and on the way, if he's as cute up close and doesn't seem like too much of a douche, we will ask him to join us for a shot in honor of the bride and groom."

"Um, no, we're not. Cade is standing right there next to him."

She grabs my arm and pulls me anyway.

Thankfully, Cash and Ashlyn arrive at the bar when we do, so instead of having to make eye contact with Cade, I'm able to congratulate the happy couple.

"I think this calls for shots!" Tory yells out.

Groomsman number three agrees. "How about some Fireball?"

"Go with tequila," Cade says. "Palmer is allergic to cinnamon."

Surprised he remembers, my gaze flickers toward his gorgeous blue eyes. When he meets my stare, I turn away. I have to stop looking at him. It's like I'm stuck in one of those bad dreams where something is just outside your reach. In this case, I'm standing on opposite sides of a glass door, staring at the most gorgeous man I've ever seen, but every time I try to open the door to be with him, I find the door is locked. Which is fitting. The door to Cade and me together is permanently locked, and I'm sure he purposely threw away the key. Actually, he probably torched the key and melted it down to nothing, so it could never, ever be used to unlock that door again.

And I deserve that.

The group gathers around the bar, minus Cash and Ashlyn, who move on to greet more guests.

"I'm Tory," she says, holding her hand out to groomsman number three. "If we're going to do shots together, we need to know each other's names."

"This seems like a no-names kind of night," he laughs. "In honor of the bride and groom."

"I don't get it," Tory says.

"Haven't you heard the story or seen the video of how Cash and Ashlyn met?"

"I saw the video from *The Elle Show* of how he proposed," Tory admits, but then she lies. "But I don't really know the whole backstory. I'm the plus one."

The groomsman glances at Tory's perky boob job, which is prominently on display in her low-cut, bronze cocktail dress, and apparently he decides she's worth telling the story to.

"It just so happens," he says, "that the bride and groom met at a wedding, just like we are now. They got drunk, hooked up, flew to Vegas, and got married. They didn't tell each other their real names."

"How could Cash not have known who Ashlyn Roberts is?" Tory inquires. "She's pretty famous."

I'm trying very hard to pretend to be enthralled with their conversation, but I can feel Cade's eyes on me.

"He knew who she was, but she didn't know who he was," the groomsman continues.

"But his brother, Cade, is her agent. Cash looks like him." Tory is playing dumb to keep the guy talking. She totally knows this entire story.

The groomsman waves his hand. "Doesn't matter. They figured it out, and now we are here at their wedding." He passes around the shots and says, "To a no-names kind of night."

We clink our glasses together then down the shots. The groomsman passes me a lime wedge, but I shake my head, causing him to pull me aside.

"My name's Jared," he says with a cocky smirk.

"I thought this was supposed to be a no-names night?" I reply, giving him shit, even though I have no interest in him.

"It is. But for you, I'll make an exception. You need to know what name to say when I make you scream later."

Cade comes up from behind Jared, clamping his big hand down on Jared's skinny shoulder.

Jared glances back at Cade. They share some kind of a look that causes Jared to immediately ditch me. He saunters over to Tory and throws his arm around her, which earns him a hint of a smile from Cade.

"So does this mean you're not married?" Tory asks Jared.

"Nope, I'm single as a Pringle," he replies.

I expect Cade to say something to me, but instead he turns away.

I'm not sure what just happened, but I think it was some guy-code thing.

And it pisses me off.

Tory sees the rage on my face, takes my hand, and drags me off to the bathroom.

"What's wrong?"

"Did you see that!?" I rant, as we step inside the ladies' room, finding a long line. "Cade cock blocked me! Not that I wanted that guy's cock, because you already called dibs on it, but Cade didn't know that!"

"Since you don't have a cock," she replies. "I think it's called *blocking the box*."

"Oh, no," the girl in front of us says. "It's called *twat blocking*."

"I thought it was *boxed*," another woman says.

"Baseball players call cock blocking *stealing signs*."

A voice from inside one of the stalls yells out, "It's called *clam jamming*."

Pretty soon everyone in the bathroom is giving us their opinions.

*"Twat swatting or twat stopping."*

*"Beaver dammed."*

*"Va-jected!"*

I shake my head at Tory. "Whatever. It really shouldn't matter what part you have. I got cock blocked because I will be having *no* cock tonight."

"There's still time," Tory says. "You can have the groomsman. You need to get laid worse than I do, honey. It's been far too long."

"But why would he cock block me and then walk away?!"

As soon as the words tumble out of my mouth, Cade's mother steps out of one of the stalls.

I put my head down, hoping she won't notice me and, thankfully, she squeezes past us without saying a word.

"Holy buckets," Tory says when the door closes behind her. "Wasn't that his mother?"

"Uh, yeah. You can kill me now."

BY THE TIME we get back from the ladies' room, everyone is being seated for dinner in the elaborately decorated ballroom. We find our table assignment then discover we're seated next to Jared—who probably switched our cards—along with a group of he and Cash's rowdy fraternity brothers.

The dinner conversation is bawdy and fun. The toast Carter gives is heartfelt and funny. Dinner is four courses of deliciousness. Then we watch as the happy couple shares their first dance and then as they cut the cake.

Tory and I immediately head straight for the cake while the boys opt for the bar, promising to bring us back more shots.

"Tell me why you broke up," Tory says. She wasn't my assistant back then, and I've never told her. It's not something I like to talk about, and I usually avoid the subject.

But tonight I comply.

Must be the shots.

"I got my first big break in a starring role. The contract had a nudity clause. I said yes. Cade said no. We fought about it. Broke up. End of story."

"That's not the end of the story," Tory says, putting a forkful of cake in her mouth. "I see the way you look at him."

"If I had a shrink, he'd probably tell me I'm standing in the way of my own happiness. That I need to let go of the guilt I feel about it. It's just that when we broke up— even though I was the one who did the breaking—it destroyed me. I hated myself. Hated him. But, mostly, I hated my heart. I think I'm still grieving. I've dated since then but never had more than a casual relationship. And it doesn't help that he's an agent. That he's hot. That we seem to end up at a lot of the same events and parties. It's like a constant reminder of my idiocy."

"Take a bite of cake," she says. "It's divine. Remind me again—when was the last time you ended up at an event together. The time before Fashion Week." I roll my eyes. She knows the answer to her question. Probably wrote it on my calendar. She grins at me then snaps her finger like she just remembered. "Oh, I know. We both saw him at that charity 10K. He ran, right?"

"Yeah," I say flatly. "He and Carter ran in it together."

"Those boys shirtless. Jogging. It was better than a Chippendales show. Remember the way all those women were gawking at their muscles? You'd think they had their dollar bills ready."

"If I recall, you were the one taking photos of their abs from afar."

She giggles. "Those Crawford boys are scrumptious. I'd like to take a bite out of—"

"Tory!"

"I'm just saying. Hard to believe no one has snagged them yet."

"Well, one did. Ashlyn. Thus, the wedding..."

"Whatever, all I know is we are going out for the bouquet toss."

"You can take part in that craziness," I tell her. "I'm not. That's the last thing I want to do."

"Oh, yes you are. Even if I have to drag your ass out there."

"You can drag me, but I'm not even going to attempt to catch it. I shouldn't even be here. This is ridiculous. I brought a gift. Made an appearance. Let's go."

"We're not going anywhere. One of us is getting laid

tonight. And if you don't want Jared, I'll take him for myself. I'm pretty sure he wants to get naughty, and I think mama can teach that boy a thing or two."

Tory glances behind me and grins.

I turn to see what she's looking at, expecting to see a hot guy, but instead finding Cade's mother approaching us. I look for a way to escape, but I can't find one.

"Palmer, it's so good to see you," she says, giving me a warm embrace.

"Thank you, Mrs. Crawford."

"It's been too long since we've seen both you and that handsome brother of yours. We've had to resort to watching your movies and seeing Pike play baseball on TV. It's just not the same."

"I've just been—" I glance at Cade, whose eyes I can feel from across the room. "Um—"

"Busy?" she asks.

"Yes, *work* has kept me busy." I shove cake in my mouth, hoping she won't say anything else.

"Just because you fired Cade as your agent, doesn't mean you can't still be friends. Our families were friends for years. I'm glad you're here, dear. Who did you bring with you? Are you dating anyone?"

"Uh, no," I fumble over my words. Mostly because Cade just winked at me. It's an old habit—something he did even before we dated—when I was starting out in the movie industry. When people thought I was just an airhead model. It used to give me confidence. Now, it simply unravels me. "I brought my, uh, my friend—"

"I'm Tory," Tory finally says, extending her hand. "Palmer's assistant. Delighted to meet you."

"Very nice to meet you, too, Tory. Oh, look. They're getting ready to do the garter and bouquet toss." She pushes both Tory and I out onto the dance floor. "Go on. It's a silly tradition, but everyone can use a little luck in the dating scene these days—what with Tinder and all those hooking up apps. It's no wonder a man doesn't want to marry."

Tory and I end up in a group of single women.

"Guess we're both going out to catch the bouquet," Tory quips.

Cash leads Ashlyn out to the center of the dance floor where she sits in a chair. Cash drops to his knees and starts digging through the fluffy layers of Ashlyn's ball gown. When he finds the garter, he gives her a naughty smirk—one that looks exactly like Cade's—leans down and sexily pulls it off with his teeth.

The frat boys all go nuts, cheering and whistling.

Cash shoots the garter up into the air, and I watch as it literally drops into Cade's hands. Like, he didn't even try to catch it.

"Shit. Now I *have* to catch the bouquet," I mutter.

"If catching it means I get that ridiculously hand-some man for myself," Tory says, "I'll fight you for it. I'd cut a bitch for a piece of that."

"You can't go against me, Tory! Besides, look at all the women eyeing him now. And that one—" I point, "—she's giving him flirty eyes. She needs to stop that!"

Tory pushes me into the center of the dance floor as Ashlyn takes her place, turns her back toward us, and tosses the bouquet high into the air.

I'm tall, and my brother used to make me play catch with him in the backyard. Screw Miss Bedroom Eyes, he's mine.

I jump up, stretching my body out like I'm going up for a pop fly to center field.

A flower hits my hand, I grasp it with all my might, and come down with it.

"Woot!" Tory yells, cheering me on. The rest of the girls let out a collective sigh, scowl at me, and then disperse.

The wedding photographer grabs me by the arm. "We need a photo of you with the guy who caught the garter." She drags me over toward Cade, telling him the same and pushing us together.

"That was quite the leap," Cade says to me.

"You didn't even try. The garter pretty much fell into your hands."

"You know what this means, right?" the photographer asks. "You two will be the next to get married."

I look into Cade's beautiful blue eyes. Eyes that

haunt my soul. Eyes that invade my dreams. Eyes I thought would be my future.

"I wouldn't bet on that, Delilah," Cade replies to the photographer. And I swear, he's flirting with her. Is he hitting on her in front of me? After he just cock blocked me? What the fuck?

"Cade is a perennial bachelor," I say, wanting to wipe that smile off her face. "*No* woman will ever tie him down."

Cade puts his hand across the small of my back and leans in toward me, his touch causing me to jump.

"One woman did, once," he whispers, going a step further and pulling me completely into his arms.

Goosebumps instantly form, even though I feel quite flush.

"Are you cold?" he asks, sliding his hands up and down my arms to warm me.

"Yeah, ocean breeze, I guess." A stupid thing to say since we are inside a ballroom.

"Okay," the photographer says. "Smile and say, *I'm getting married soon!*"

Cade reaches out and brushes his finger down my cheek. "You just have a little frosting—"

I gulp when he touches me.

Neither of us is paying any attention to the photographer. We're just gazing at each other, our eyes locked, conveying words we don't dare to speak. I haven't been in his arms in years, but it feels like the most natural thing in the world. Like our breakup never happened. He glances at my lips, causing me to lick them and tilt my head upward in anticipation of his kiss.

"I need you to look at *me*," the photographer growls, snatching away our brief but beautiful moment.

Cade and I turn toward the camera and smile.

She clicks and leaves.

"You winked at me—from across the room," I stutter.

"Old habit, sorry," he states. "Nice to see you, Palmer, and good luck with the bouquet."

# October 16th
## *Pike*

"HEY, PEACHES," I say, using the nickname I've called my little sister since she was a kid.

"Hey, Pike! Are you on your way to Texas? Can I come to the game?"

"You came to the playoffs two years ago, and we didn't make it to the big game. I want you to wait and come when I pitch in the first game of the World Series. It's my year. I can feel it."

"I'm so happy for you, Pike. It was hard on all of us when L.A. traded you to Tampa."

"To have them practically blame me for losing the playoffs after playing there for most of my career was a blow. But Tampa took a shot on me even knowing I needed shoulder surgery. We have a great team. Seriously, sis, I feel good about our chances. So put Tuesday, October the twenty-eighth on your calendar."

"Is your shoulder really holding up?"

"It is. I know I'm getting old for a pitcher, but at thirty-four, I'm in the best shape of my life. And for the first time in years I'm not in pain with every pitch."

"And how are things with Britney?"

"It's Bethany. And she's pushing to get married."

"And you're resisting as usual?"

"I'm not convinced I want to spend the rest of my life with her. Speaking of that, do you ever see Cameron?"

"She was in Milan for Fashion Week. We had lunch."

"How is she?"

"Maybe you should call her and ask her that yourself."

"Did she ask about me?"

"Pike, you dated her off and on for almost a decade. Every time she stops dating someone, the tabloids wonder if the two of you will get back together. Of course she asked about you."

"And?"

"We just talked about life and love, fashion, and the movie industry. She's close to wrapping up the movie she's working on and then she's taking a few months off—going to her place in Hawaii to just surf and chill."

"Is she seeing anyone?"

"If that's what you really wanted to know, why didn't you just ask me that in the first place?"

"Just answer the question," I say.

"No, she's not. Not seriously, anyway. She says lately

she's had a string of bad dates, and she's given up. But she said it in that way she does. She's so animated and funny. We laughed all through lunch."

"She always made me laugh, too."

"Maybe you should call her and catch up."

"I gotta get through this season, first. Then, maybe. But I have to be honest. I like living in Florida. It's quiet and people respect my privacy—as opposed to when I was in L.A. where the tours buses drove by my house. Maybe I'll settle down and buy a place on the Gulf."

"Settle down—like retire?"

"Not for a few more years."

"You and Cade always joked that when you made the big leagues you were going to share a house like the Playboy Mansion." She laughs. My sister has a beautiful laugh. One that always makes me feel happy. But hearing Cade's name immediately pisses me off.

"Asshole," I say.

"I saw him a few days ago. Ashlyn Roberts married his brother, Cash. I went to the wedding."

"Carter told me about that. I see him quite a bit. He's the agent for a kid on my team. I actually called him for advice on my last contract. I felt like Jimmy had been my agent for so long that he was just phoning it in."

"I danced with Carter at the wedding."

"How is their family?

"They're doing well."

"That's good. Dad and Mr. Crawford were good friends and important men in my life growing up."

"I still miss Dad, and I hate that Mom moved to Palm Springs."

"The house in Laguna was too big for her, and with you and I always gone, I can see why she wanted to move. She loves it there."

"Make sure you call her on Sunday. She doesn't like when you forget."

"I know," I say. "And I will. Good to talk to you, sis."

"Can I wish you good luck in the playoffs? Or should I say break a leg like we do in my profession?"

"What did you tell me last time?"

"I wished you good luck."

"Then let's go with the other."

"Break a leg, Pike," she says.

# October 24th
## *Cade*

MY WHOLE FAMILY is in Cabo San Lucas staying at my parents' villa in Palmilla. Usually we are here earlier in the year, but with Cash and Ashlyn's wedding and honeymoon, we moved the date out.

We're camped out in the sand, soaking up the sun.

The newlyweds are snuggled up together on a chaise, and can't seem to keep their hands off each other. It makes me feel both jealous and slightly nauseous.

"Ashlyn, the wedding turned out spectacular," Mom says. "One Crawford child down, three more to go. Then we can get on to the important part—grandchildren. I'm desperate for them. All my friends already have grand-babies. This family has got some catching up to do."

"I'm pregnant, Mom," Chloe says nonchalantly as she sprays sunblock on her arms.

"You're *what*?!" Mom exclaims. "Tell me it's not by the pizza delivery boy!"

Chloe gives Mom a tight-lipped smile. "Guess you aren't quite *that* desperate yet."

"That is *not* funny, Chloe."

"I thought it was pretty funny," Cash says, laughing.

Chloe high-fives him. She has no desire to settle down anytime in the near future, choosing rather to work on growing her jewelry business and travel the world. She went to Paris this year for inspiration and is currently planning a trip to Tuscany.

Mom turns to Ashlyn. "So, Ashlyn, have you and Cash talked about when you're going to have children?"

"Yes, actually. We were thinking in a few years. I have two movies to do—thanks to your sons—a gorgeously newly decorated home—thanks to you and Cash—and feel like my life is finally in order. Cash and I want to travel a little and spend some time as a couple, then we'll work on a family."

"So you weren't upset we decorated one of the bedrooms as a nursery?"

"No, just the opposite. We're excited it's already done. And just think, when we do have a baby we can tell him it was decorated with love from Grandma."

"That's so sweet," Mom says, clearly delighted at the prospect of it.

Ashlyn's phone vibrates on the table next to her. She looks at it and then glances at me and frowns. Then she shows Cash.

"Work?" I ask. Ashlyn is one of my clients.

"Uh, um," she hesitates. "A friend saw a picture I

posted. She's in town and wants to get together."

"Is that bad?"

"It's not," Cash answers.

"Oh. The way you looked, I just thought—"

"Nothing bad for us anymore," Cash says, taking Ashlyn's hand in his and kissing it.

And he's right, in the short time since Ashlyn met Cash, she's gone from the star I was afraid was going to burn out and fade away, to model client.

"We should all go," Mom suggests.

"I don't think we were invited, Mom."

"Not to change the subject," Carter says, changing the subject, "Vale will be here tomorrow night."

"Is she in town, too?" I ask.

"She's been doing a shoot in Costa Rica and thought she'd drop by."

"I thought she only called you at night, Carter, for the *boot-tay*," Cash teases.

Mom perks up. "She *booty* calls him?"

"I'm sure she just enjoys his company," Dad says, trying to cover for Carter, but Mom's not having it.

"That seems a little forward."

"I'm calling bullshit!" Dad laughs. "I seem to recall a certain young sorority girl who would call a strapping football player at night when she got tired of drunk frat boys hitting on her."

"Mom!" Carter laughs. "You booty-called Dad?"

"I most certainly did not," she says, but Dad raises an eyebrow in her direction. "Fine. I may have called him once after a frat party, but it wasn't for that. We were friends."

Cash, Ashlyn, and Chloe burst out laughing. "That's what Carter says about Vale!"

I can't help but laugh, too. This is why I love my family and why at my age I still go on vacation with them every year.

LATER, CARTER AND I are drinking beers together on the pool deck. Everyone else is in the house getting dinner ready. We tried to help, but Mom shooed us out, saying there were too many cooks in the kitchen.

"More like too many cocks," Ashlyn had quipped under her breath, making Carter and I laugh.

"To family vacations," Carter says, clinking my bottle.

"So, what's the deal with Vale?"

"We hook up. It's fantastic, but it's supposed to just be fun. Nothing serious."

"But you want more than that?"

He runs his hand through his hair in frustration. "She travels a lot. Says she doesn't want to be in a serious relationship, but when we're together, it feels like it could be serious."

"How did you meet her again?"

"Super Bowl party last year. We got teamed up in a video game contest. She beat me."

"Did you let her win?"

"No, I just—she was beautiful, you know. It was hard to concentrate."

"Fell hard fast?"

"Pretty girls don't fluster me," he says. "But she sure did. She's beautiful and all, but she's cute, too."

"The girl every boy wishes they could have grown up next door to."

"I would have been spanking it every day. It would have been torture," he laughs.

"Oh, give me a break," I say, slapping him on the back. "The quarterback always gets the girl."

"I'm not the quarterback anymore. It's weird how your life changes. I thought for sure I'd be playing pro ball now. It's all I worked toward growing up."

"You used to tell us you were going to be on TV every Sunday."

"Until the injury that ended my career."

"Yeah, well, when they carted you off on a backboard, none of us were worried about your career, Carter. We were worried about your life. It was a violent collision that broke your back in three places. You're lucky you weren't paralyzed."

"I know. Life has worked out well for me, regardless. I love being a sports agent. I've done very well, so it's not that I'm complaining, really, but part of me wonders if I was if Vale would fall for me."

"If she would fall for you just because you were a professional quarterback, you shouldn't want her."

"I know." He sighs.

"Have you told her how you feel?"

"No. I don't want to mess up a good thing. Or scare her away."

"If you love her, Carter, you should tell her."

"I feel like I'm on the scout team with her."

"And you want to be the starter?"

"Yeah," he admits.

"Is she seeing other people? Are you?"

"In the last month, I haven't. I don't know about her. She's been traveling nonstop since New York Fashion Week. We talk most every day, but she could have a different guy in every country, for all I know."

"When you see her tomorrow, you should ask her."

"Maybe."

"You aren't going to, are you?"

"No, not yet. I don't want to screw things up."

"Do you ever think about getting married?" I ask him. It has been on my mind since I saw Palmer at the wedding.

"Our brother is certainly happy," he says, glancing inside at the newlyweds, who are wrapped in each other's arms, kissing.

"Cash was always a serial dater," I counter. "Unlike you."

He grins, recalling his glory days. "I did get a lot of tail in college."

"One of the benefits of being a star collegiate quarterback."

"Or the star catcher. Remember those shirts all the girls wore when you and Pike were playing together? My goal in life when I was in high school was to someday have stands full of girls wearing my name."

"The *I got Piked* shirts?"

"If I recall, many said *Caught by Cade.*"

"Well, back then there *was* a lot of juggling the lineup." I laugh and take a pull of my beer.

"Seems like there's still a lot of juggling of the lineup for you. Be honest with me, do you wish you were hitting home runs with the same girl every night?"

I glance in the house. Ashlyn is now lying on the couch with her head in Cash's lap. He's stroking her hair gently as they talk. "They do look happy," I admit. And I was happy like that once, too.

"After Cash and his long-time girlfriend broke up, he was a lot like us, playing the field," Carter states. "Until he met Ashlyn."

"Exactly my point," I say. "You never know when it will hit you. He was hoping to get laid, and now look at him."

"So, you're saying there's hope for me and Vale?"

"I'm saying you never know."

"She's like a guy when it comes to sex. I'm not quite sure how to handle her. Speaking of not handling her, what are you going to do about Palmer?"

"Nothing. She's part of my past. Honestly, I was thinking about Jules. You know we've been good friends for a while now, and she's always been a great date when I need one. I think she likes me."

Carter laughs. "You're so full of it. Jules got engaged last month."

"To who? How long has she known this guy?"

"To Todd."

"From college, Todd?"

"Yeah, once you and Pike stopped being friends, you sort of dropped out of—"

"Whatever. How did they end up together?"

"She stayed friends with Pike. So did Todd. They were all at a party together, say they both knew, and got engaged after just a few months of dating. They're crazy about each other." He smirks at me. "There goes your plan."

"You're one to talk. What if Vale is seeing someone else? What if that guy acts first?"

He shakes his head. "I don't even want to think about it. Same could be said about Palmer. Maybe I should invite her to join us, too."

"Don't you fucking dare," I reply, with a pointed look. "It's our family vacation. I don't want to ruin it."

Cash leaves his bride and joins us on the deck, setting down an ice-filled bucket of beers and saying, "Can you believe Mom booty-called Dad?"

We all laugh.

# October 25th
## *Cade*

WE'RE AT A quaint little Mexican restaurant, getting ready to have a late lunch when Palmer walks in.

"What the hell is she doing here?" I mutter.

"She's in town doing a photo shoot for a designer," Ashlyn answers.

"No one talk to her," I say. "Maybe she won't see us."

"Don't be ridiculous, Cade," Mom scolds. "I raised you better than that."

"Palmer," Dad says, standing up. "How wonderful to see you again. You look well."

Palmer turns and looks toward our table and says, "Thank you. So do you."

"Retirement suits me. Are you meeting someone here?"

"I, uh—"

Ash leans over and whispers to Cash, "She's rambling. It's cute."

"It's not cute," I disagree. "It's awkward."

"Then why are you looking at her like you're a dog and she's a bone? No, actually, like she's a bacon, barbecue, and meat-sauce-smothered bone," Cash asks.

"I am not," I snarl, wondering why I'm so worked up about her being here. Probably because I'm pissed. Not one single person in my family looks surprised to see her.

"Is Palmer who you were texting yesterday?" I ask Ashlyn.

She ignores me, instead getting up and giving Palmer a hug.

"I'm so glad you could join us," she says, confirming what I thought.

What the fuck?

I glare at Cash and Carter, who both give me smirks. If Mom and Dad weren't sitting here, I'd wipe those smug looks right off their faces.

"I didn't realize the whole family was here," Palmer says, her eyes landing on me. She was clearly blindsided too. "This isn't your usual week."

"With the engagement, planning, and wedding taking place over such a short period, we didn't have time for a getaway," Mom says, standing to greet Palmer. "Cash and Ashlyn are just back from their honeymoon. You must join us." She points to the seat she just vacated. "You can sit here."

"Oh, I don't want to intrude," she says to Mom, even though her eyes are locked on mine. "I'll just sit at the bar and grab a quick bite. Ashlyn and I can catch up later."

"Nonsense, Palmer," Mom says in a firm tone. "Sit."

Ashlyn grabs Palmer's arm and pulls her into the seat next to her, putting her directly across from me and sitting with Carter on her left.

Palmer's wearing a long, flowing dress that would reveal very little if it weren't for its very low cut, displaying her cleavage.

Carter gives her a little elbow bump when she sits down, and she smiles back at him in an intimate way.

What the hell? I stand up so quickly that I bump the table, causing my margarita to splash out of its glass.

"Carter, will you come with me for a second?" I say, trying to hide my temper.

"Why?" he asks, looking confused.

"I just got a text from a client, and I need your help with something," I reply cryptically.

"No work on vacation," Mom scolds.

"It will just take a minute," I reply, walking around the table, grabbing my brother by the shirt, and practically dragging him out of the restaurant.

"What the hell is your problem?" he says, pulling out of my grip.

"What the hell was that smile?"

"What smile?"

"The way you elbowed Palmer. The way she looked

at you. Are you *Cartering* her?"

"What the fuck? No. I told you last night I haven't been with anyone but Vale."

I ball up my fists. "Have you *ever*? I pray your answer is no, because otherwise I'm going to kill you."

Carter pushes his palm into my chest, knocking me backwards. "You need to calm the fuck down. First of all, I'm your brother. You should know better than to even ask that question."

"Cash was sleeping with Ashlyn behind my back."

"To my knowledge, you had never slept with her. Big difference."

"Are you saying you've never slept with anyone I've slept with?"

"Only once, but I didn't know it until after."

"What do you mean?"

"She said, *Two Crawford brothers down, one to go.* I was pissed."

"Did you warn Cash?"

"Yeah, I did. Because that's what brothers do. If my elbowing Palmer upsets you that much, you need to do something about it."

I narrow my eyes at him. "You weren't surprised to see her."

"No, I wasn't," he says, leaving me standing in the street.

I follow him back inside and to our table.

"Did you get your business done?" Mom asks in a way that lets me know I better have.

"Yeah," Carter says, taking his seat. "One of his clients *desperately* needed box seats for one of the playoff games. I was able to help."

"Well, since we all have our drinks, let's toast." Cash holds up his cactus-stemmed margarita glass. "To family."

"To family," everyone says.

I touch my glass to Palmer's and meet her gaze.

## *Palmer*

CADE GETS UP to use the restroom. I wait a few moments, then excuse myself to use the ladies' room.

I lean against the wall in the hallway, thankful it's hidden from the table's view.

"I had no idea you were going to be here," I tell him when he walks out of the mens' room.

"I could tell by the look on your face," he says, his presence making the hallway seen smaller than it is. It's hard to be this close to him and not just sink into his arms.

"I think Ashlyn is trying to play matchmaker," I confirm.

"It's that damn garter. It literally fell into my hand. I wasn't even trying." He leans closer to me. "You, on the other hand . . ."

"My competitive side took over," I admit, shaking my head. "Or maybe it was the tequila shots."

He laughs. It's deep and sexy.

And way too familiar.

*I'm lying in bed, tangled up in the sheets, the morning after my twenty-first birthday with none other than Cade Crawford. After years of lusting after him, after years of excuses—you're too young, your brother is my best friend, you're my client—it finally happened.*

*We were both a little drunk when we got back to my place, frantic with need, our desire great. As the night progressed, the sex seemed to morph from a hot-mess hook-up to sweet lovemaking, the likes of which I have never experienced.*

*He stirs, wraps his arm tightly around me, and pulls me closer. His lips are against my temple as he whispers, "You better remember last night, because I'll never forget it."*

*"I don't know, Cade. I was pretty drunk," I tease.*

*He chuckles, deep and sexy, but looks at me seriously. "Tell me the truth."*

*I let out a contented sigh, still basking in the beauty of it. "It was the best night of my life."*

"Palmer?"

"Uh, what?"

"I said we better get back out there before anyone gets any ideas about us."

"Oh, yeah. Right."

AFTER A DELICIOUS meal and quite a few pitchers of margaritas, Mrs. Crawford says, "Palmer, dear, you must come back to the house with us."

"I, um—"

"I'm making brownies."

Ashlyn, who's a bit tipsy, wraps her arm around my neck. "She's teaching me how to make the Crawford family secret recipe."

"You always loved my brownies when you were a girl, Palmer," Mrs. Crawford says. "Although, I try to keep the recipe in the family, I do occasionally make exceptions. And since you caught the bouquet at the wedding"—she goes on, while I silently curse the damn thing—"you know what they say."

"What do they say?" I ask. I'm a little tipsy myself.

"The way to a man's heart is through his—"

"Dick," Chloe says under her breath, causing Ashlyn and I to giggle.

"—stomach," she continues.

"If it means we get three batches of brownies," Carter says, herding me down the beach and toward their house. "I'm all for it."

THE SUN IS hot, and by the time we walk through the sand the few blocks to their house, I'm sweating. Although, technically, it may be because Cade just took his shirt off.

"I think we all need to cool off in the pool," Cade says. "Cash, you're in charge of getting us some beers."

"I'm not your slave boy," Cash argues, giving his brother a backhand to the stomach. Cade doesn't flinch, just flexes his midsection, causing it to harden.

I swallow, remembering exactly how each of those muscles feels underneath my touch. *That's it, missy. No more alcohol for you.*

"I'll get the beer," their dad says. "Boys, how about some cigars, too?"

"Sounds perfect," Carter says, stripping off his shirt and running toward the pool. "Last one in is a rotten egg."

The boys barrel past each other, laughing, pushing, and clawing their way up the stairs from the beach to their villa.

"Boys," Ashlyn says, rolling her eyes.

"Never a dull moment," their mother agrees. "Why don't you girls take a swim. I normally don't drink and was thinking a little siesta sounded good. We can make the brownies later."

"Uh, okay," I say, thinking this is my chance to leave. But as I watch Cade and his brothers dive into the pool, I decide I really don't want to. Since my dad passed away, my mother has moved to Palm Springs and Pike is usually on the road. I'm enjoying this family time.

And did I mention Cade is shirtless?

Yeah, I think maybe I did.

"So who won?" Ashlyn yells as we strip off our dresses and dip our toes in the pool.

"I did!" Cash yells.

Carter throws a chokehold around his little brother's neck then dunks him under the water. "No, way! I did."

Cade sweeps his hand across the surface, launching a wall of water on Carter as Cash breaks free and comes up for air.

"Actually, Palmer was the last one in," he says, his heated gaze following the curves of my bikini-clad body. "She's the rotten egg. And you know what that means!"

I glance at Ashlyn, wondering what that means. She shrugs in my direction.

Carter jumps out of the pool, runs to the outdoor bar, grabs a bottle of tequila out of the fridge, and shakes it at me. "You get to eat the worm."

"No way!" I say, backing out of the pool.

Then I look closer at the bottle of Casa Dragones Joven, knowing it's one of the most expensive tequilas you can buy. It's my brother's personal favorite. I also happen to know there is no worm in it.

Carter brings the bottle to the pool stairs, boxing me

in between him and Cade.

"You hold her down," he says to Cade. "I'll pour."

Cade grabs me around the waist and pulls me backwards into the pool. I'm like putty in his hands, hoping he will mold me into something he'll never let go of.

But I scream. I am an actress, after all. "Ahhh! Put me down!"

Of course, he doesn't listen. Even though I kick and buck to get free, I stay firmly wrapped in his strong, muscular arms.

"You gonna make this easy or hard?" he asks.

"I want it to be hard," I sigh as he presses me tightly against his body. "Um, I mean, I'm going to make it hard. I mean—"

Cade chuckles. "I think I know exactly what you mean, you naughty little minx."

I still pretend to struggle, but mostly I'm just wiggling my ass against his torso, much like I used to when I would wake up in the morning with him spooning me. It was a sure fire way to start the morning right.

"Stop doing that," he says sternly.

"Doing what?"

His hands move down to my ass. "You're rubbing *this* against me. Don't think I don't remember your little sex tricks."

"I don't even know what you're talking about," I lie.

"You know you're turning me on. And you love it."

He pulls me tighter against him, so I can feel that he does indeed love it, but in the process is pulling me away from the tequila.

Carter swims across the pool toward us. "That's it," he says. "Don't let go of her, Cade."

Ashlyn claps and cheers. "Shots for the rotten egg!"

"Hey, you got in the same time I did."

Cash barrels out, picks Ashlyn up off the stairs, and leaps in the pool with her. They come up kissing.

I let out a sigh. It's so romantic.

"You totally ruined my hair, Cash!" she chastises, as she hugs him tighter and kisses his neck.

We watch their display of affection, going from a sweet kiss to some serious petting.

"Okay!" Carter says. "Either get a room or take a shot!" He glances at Cade and me and points his finger in our direction. "That goes for you two as well."

"What are you talking about?" Cade says, loosening his grip. "You're the one who told me to grab her."

"Uh, huh," he says, swimming out to me and holding up the bottle.

I comply, opening my mouth and allowing him to pour a long shot directly into it.

"Ashlyn's turn!" I yell.

"I had a bad tequila experience once," she says.

"This is top of the line. Honestly, we should be sipping it, not shooting it, but what the hell, we're on vacation," Carter says. "So suck it up, buttercup."

Ashlyn rolls her eyes but does the shot. The brothers then pass the bottle around, each taking a slug.

"Oh, sure, doing shots without me," Chloe says, joining us poolside with a cute guy in tow. "This is uh…" she looks at him, "tell me your name again."

"Evan."

She snaps her fingers. "That's right." Then she says to us, "Everyone, this is Evan. He makes pornos and just asked me to star in one. Can you believe my luck?"

Cade chokes on his tequila.

She strips off her dress, showing off a very skimpy bikini and numerous tattoos. "I'm just fucking with you. Evan is an assistant producer, sent here to scout a location. We just met on the beach."

She tells Evan each of our names.

"Wow, Palmer Montlake and Ashley Roberts," Evan says, "so honored to meet you both."

"It's Ashlyn Crawford," Ashlyn states. "I just got married."

Evan looks mortified.

"Evan and I need some of that tequila," Chloe says, swimming out to Cade and taking the bottle from him. She takes a gulp then gets out of the pool, taking the bottle with her. "Smell you later," she says, dragging Evan back toward the beach and flipping her brothers off in the process.

# *Cade*

AFTER MESSING AROUND in the pool, watching the brownie making class, and then having a late meal overlooking the dark ocean, Palmer thanks my parents for dinner and the brownie recipe.

"It's been lovely having you spend time with us, Palmer. We're leaving in the morning to go back home, but don't be a stranger. Cade will walk you home," Mom says, giving me a look. "I don't want her walking home alone at night."

I consider making Carter do it, but he's sulking over the fact that Vale bailed on meeting him here. Something to do with a last minute photo shoot.

I smile at my mother, who is trying to be subtle, but clearly playing matchmaker. "Of course, I'll walk her home."

Palmer hugs my siblings and Ashlyn goodbye, then we make our way down the stairs to the beach.

"It's been a great day, Cade," she says, twirling around in the sand. I always loved her spontaneity. Since we broke up, I've been living a pretty rigid life, trying to make myself feel in control. It's all an illusion though. My life only feels centered when she's in it.

I smile at her, take her hand, and we run together down the beach. Once we're panting a little, I drop to the sand on my back.

"Remember?" I ask her, throwing my hands up over my head and spreading my legs wide.

"Sand angels!" She lets out an adorable squeal and falls to her back. "What you do when there's no snow," she says, repeating what she told me then.

*She stands on her tiptoes in the sand and kisses me.*

*"It's overcast, there's a soft ocean breeze, and the beach is practically ours. It's the perfect day!" she yells as she falls straight back into the fluffy sand. I have a moment of panic, thinking she passed out or something, but she's lying on the ground with her arms in the air and a huge smile across her face. "Drop back, Cade. Make sand angels with me!"*

*"You're crazy," I tell her, laughing, then drop back and do the same, moving my arms above my head to make the wings and my feet back and forth to make the robe.*

*"Get up really carefully," she says, "so you don't ruin it."*

*I stand up carefully, meeting her back where we started.*

*"Sand angels are what you do when there's no snow."*

*"I've lived by the beach my whole life and never made a sand angel," I tease.*

*She presses her lips against mine. "I want us to experience the rest of life's firsts together, Cade."*

We both carefully stand up and move away from our angels. "After our sand angels, 'life's firsts' became sort of our couple's mantra, didn't it?" she says.

"We did a lot together. Experienced new countries,

new restaurants, new feelings. You even forced me to do one of those classes where we had to paint a picture. I must have been in love," I say with a laugh. "Good thing I didn't tell my brothers. I'm pretty sure they would have pulled my man card."

The ocean breeze blows her hair across her face as she laughs. I automatically tuck it behind her ear.

Palmer's hand grazes my forearm as I do. Her touch is like lightning on my skin, sending a jolt of regret pinging through me.

"Come on," she says, leading me to the door of her hotel. "Now you can tell your mother that I arrived safely."

I look down, my eyes landing on the lush mounds barely concealed under her dress.

Her fingers move to her collarbone and then slide down toward her cleavage. "Hard to believe this broke us up."

"That's *not* why we broke up."

"It's what started our, um, disagreement," she argues.

"No," I say hotly. "We broke up because you wouldn't listen to me. And you can be so fucking stubborn."

"Pot, meet kettle." Her face breaks out in a wide smile. The smile that always made my days brighter. "You didn't have a problem with your other clients showing their assets. You were jealous, plain and simple."

"That's not true at all. Your—never mind. It doesn't matter," I say, my hand immediately touching the spot near my hairline. "I still have the scar to prove it."

"You have a scar?" she says, standing on her tiptoes, grabbing my cheeks, and studying it.

"Well, you did throw a hot curling iron at my head," I say, causing me to drift back in time.

*"I have good news," I say, walking into my bathroom, where Palmer is curling her hair.*

*"I have better news," she says, setting the iron down, and throwing her arms around me, planting a kiss on my lips. All she's wearing are skimpy little boxer shorts and her bra. Although we're supposed to be at her mom's for dinner shortly to tell her the good news, I'm thinking we may have to be a little late.*

*"My brother is in town! He's coming to dinner tonight. We can tell them both!" She pulls back, holding out her left hand and gazing at the sparkling diamond engagement ring I slid on her finger this weekend when she said yes.*

*I back away, sitting on the edge of the tub. "I was hoping to tell your mom first," I say. Her brother, Pike, my long-time best friend, doesn't know I've been seeing his little sister behind his back. "He's not going to be happy for us. He's going to be pissed."*

*"You've wanted to tell him since our first date six months ago, now all of a sudden you're scared? Don't worry, Cade. He'll be fine about it."*

*"No, Palmer, he won't be. I can't believe I ever let you talk me into hiding our relationship. Especially from my best friend."*

*"It hasn't been that hard. He travels all the time."*

*"I still feel guilty every time I talk to him."*

*"Cade, seriously. I'm an adult, and I can date whoever I want."*

*"That's not the issue. The issue is that we have been lying about it."*

She leans against the counter, looking sexier than ever. I really don't want to fight with her about this. I'm dying to tell her my good news. *"Never once have we lied about it."*

*"Lying by omission is just as bad."*

She rolls her eyes then turns her back to me, picking up the curling iron and wrapping a strand of hair around it, ignoring the subject. Our relationship is complicated because I've been friends with her brother since high school, which is exactly why when we were just hooking up in the beginning, she didn't want him to know.

*"Once we started dated exclusively, we should have told him."* I run my hand through my hair, pushing it back, knowing he's going to kill me and now not looking forward to tonight.

She looks at me in the mirror, while she curls another strand and argues, *"But I didn't want to. I didn't want him lecturing me about dating my agent. About dating his best friend. If he gets pissed, just blame me. I'll take it. I can deal with my brother."*

"It's not that I can't deal with him. It's the fact that I asked you to marry me without asking for your family first. That's not the way I was raised. If your dad was still alive, I would have asked him." And I would have. On his deathbed he told me to take care of his girl. I never knew if he meant take care of her from a career standpoint or if he could tell there was more between us.

Tears fill her eyes. "I still can't believe Dad's gone," she says. Her dad passed away three months ago, after discovering he had stage four pancreatic cancer. I had convinced her to tell her family about us just before we got the news about his diagnosis. She was devastated and said she couldn't deal with it. When I would push the subject, she'd break down crying, and I felt like an ass. And as much as it is a subject of contention between us, everything else about us is amazing. Deep down, I don't want to rock the boat either.

I am stupidly in love with this girl.

My mom says that love knows no boundaries, and I suppose this is true.

"So what's your good news?" she asks, changing the subject.

"I got a contract today for the movie you auditioned for. You got it, baby! They want you for the starring role."

"Oh my God! Are you serious!" She sets the iron down and throws her arms around me again. "What an amazing week! First we get engaged and now this! Can you believe this? It's my dream, Cade!"

"I'm your agent. Of course, I can believe it. You're

*beautiful, talented, and funny. This role was made for you."*

*I give her a long congratulatory kiss. "There could be one little catch, but I'll take care of it."*

*"What catch?"*

*"They requested a nudity clause. I told them no, of course."*

*"You what?! Why would you do that without asking me first?!" Her face turns red; she has a quick temper like her brother. I stay calm.*

*"Part of my job and why you should have an agent negotiate for you—is because you're too emotionally involved. Besides, we agreed early on that you wouldn't do that. You said it's what you wanted." And it's also what I promised her brother, when he came to me after she'd gotten her first small role and asked me to be her agent.*

*"So they want me to get naked? Like completely?"*

*"The clause calls for a shot of sideboob in a love scene."*

*"Sideboob? That's it?"*

*"It's a little more than that. In the movie, it will look like you're making love. You'll be sitting on top of your co-star. They asked for a naked side shot from the waist up. I told them it was nonnegotiable."*

*"Why would you do that? This is my big break, Cade! What if they change their minds and don't want me?"*

*"Then we find another movie to do."*

*"It's not that easy. Do you know how many auditions I've been to? How many roles I've missed out on? I want you to call them back right now and tell them I'll do it. I was a*

model, Cade. It's not like people have never seen the side of my boob before."

"I realize that, but this has a different context. It's a sex scene. Your boob will be against your co-star. Of course, they would put a flesh-toned pastie over your nipples, but still. And—"

"Is that what this is all about?" she yells, angry tears forming. "You just don't want me to do this movie because you're jealous! It's acting, Cade. If you can't deal with me doing love scenes then we shouldn't get married!"

"I'll deal with it. I promise. I'm a good negotiator, and I'll get them to take it out. Calm down."

"Don't tell me to calm down. Don't you dare. I'm signing it. Give me the contract. Now!"

"No, you're not."

"You can't tell me what to do."

"I'm your agent. I'm supposed to help guide your career."

"You're not acting like my agent! You're acting like a stupid jealous boyfriend! Do you not understand what this means to me?"

"Fiancée," I correct. "This is business, Palmer, not personal. This is what you told me were your priorities since I took you on as a client. Think about how your dad would have felt if you did a scene like—"

"Oh, don't you fucking dare bring my dad into this!" Tears pour down her face. "You're being a jealous asshole!"

I try to pull her into my arms, but she throws her arms

up in the air, blocking me. "Don't touch me. Either agree with me or you're fired."

"Palmer, I don't think we'll lose the deal over it, or I never would have told you about it."

"Not told me about the deal of a lifetime? I can't even believe you'd be willing to risk my career over a fucking sideboob!"

"Palmer, there will be other movies if this isn't the right one."

"I want to do this movie. This movie is my big break. It's everything."

"Not this way."

"Fuck you, Cade! You're fired!" She throws the curling iron in my direction. I duck, but the hot barrel pings against my forehead and tumbles to the ground as she storms out of the room, crying.

I run after her. I just need to calm her down so we can discuss this rationally.

I round the corner into the hall and see her reaching for the knob on the front door.

"Palmer, don't go!" I yell.

She takes off her engagement ring and sets it on the table. "I'm sorry, Cade. I can't marry someone who doesn't support my career."

Then she storms out the door, jumps in her car, and drives away.

I stand still, looking down at the ring. The ring that

*represents my future happiness.*

*I take a deep breath.*

*She's just mad. She'll calm down. We'll talk tomorrow. Have amazing make-up sex. Everything will be okay.*

*But as I pick up the ring and hold it in my hand, I have a moment of doubt. Was I wrong? Could I ruin her career before it really gets started over something so stupid as a sideboob? If she was any one of my other clients, I would have been fine with the clause.*

*But I didn't promise the brother of any other client what I promised hers.*

*I put the two-point-six carat, brilliant cut solitaire ring that is encircled by another carat of quadrillion diamonds carefully on my nightstand. Tomorrow, I'll put the ring back on her finger, even if it means going against her brother's wishes. It sounds horrible of me to say about my best friend, but I'd rather have him mad at me than her unhappy.*

*My phone rings.*

*I immediately answer, thinking it's her.*

*"Hey, meet us at Lure," my friend Todd says.*

*I am really not in the mood to hang out, but I need a drink. Badly.*

*I lock up my condo and head down the street. I'll have one drink, give her time to calm down, then call her. I can't wait until morning. I can't go to sleep knowing she's mad at me. I need to fix this tonight.*

*It's a short walk from my condo on Laguna Beach to our*

*favorite watering hole, but as the salt air clears my head, and the ocean breeze fills me with memories of long days spent on the beach with her, I change my mind again.*

*I'm not waiting. I'm going now.*

"Cade, my man," Todd says, giving me a slap on the back. *I hadn't even realized I was standing outside the bar already.* "The gang's all gonna be here tonight. Pike's in town, and he's stopping by."

*I glance at my phone, noticing that he texted me earlier saying the same.*

*What I don't have is a text from Palmer.*

"Uh, hang on, Todd. I need to make a quick call."

"Hopefully whoever you're calling is blonde, stacked, and has a lot of hot friends. The boys are back in town!" *he yells as he herds me inside and orders us beers.*

*I step away from the bar and hit Palmer's number. It rings and rings, then goes to voicemail. I hang up and try again.*

*Still no answer.*

*This time, I leave a message.* "Palmer, please call me so we can talk about this."

*I hang up, knowing that was the wrong thing to say. I should have said* I love you and nothing else matters. *I set my phone down on the bar and chug my beer. I'll finish this, then go tell her in person.*

*Todd slaps me on the back and starts recalling nights out of town traveling to tournaments for our select baseball team.*

"*Remember those chicks in the hot tub at the hotel in San Antonio?*" he says, then goes off on a three-minute discussion of it.

A bunch of the other guys from the team join us. We're exchanging greetings and reminiscing when Pike storms into the bar.

"*You son of bitch!*" Pike yells as he charges toward me then throws a punch at my face. "*How could you do that?*"

The blow knocks me back against the bar, and I fumble trying to steady myself. But I don't get time to recover. Pike slams his fist into my stomach. "*I trusted you like a brother!*"

"*What the hell?*" our friend Todd says, stepping between us and holding out his arms to keep the peace. "*You're best friends. What's this all about?*"

A livid Pike shoves Todd out of the way, knocking him to the ground. "*What this is about is my best friend sleeping with my sister behind my back.*"

"*I can explain,*" I say as his fist connects with my face again, this time cutting open my lip.

"*There's nothing to explain, you cocksucker! You fucked with my sister!*"

"*I wanted to tell you, Pike.*" I hold up my hands in an attempt to protect myself. "*But she wouldn't let me!*"

"*That's a bullshit answer. We're best friends. Brothers. You betrayed me!*"

He's right. I did.

"*And then you broke her heart!*" he yells furiously, slamming me with a fast barrage of punches that connect *with my temple, ribs, stomach, jaw, and then nose.*

*I don't even try to stop him. I deserve this.*

*With the last punch, I spin in a circle and fall to the ground.*

*Pike glares down at me and spits on my shirt. "If you ever come near my sister again, I'll fucking kill you."*

*Then he turns and storms out of the bar.*

*The disgusted looks on our friends' faces rain down on me.*

*I lay on the bar floor and close my eyes, both my body and heart feeling completely broken.*

"I'm sorry, Cade," she says, gently grazing her fingers across the scar and bringing me back to the present. She gives me a little frown then turns on her heel and goes into the hotel.

As I WALK down the beach alone, I realize that even after all these years I'm still broken. Because she's not in my life.

# October 26th
## *Palmer*

AFTER DOING THE pre-dawn photo shoot for the designer who does most of my red carpet gowns, I fly home, unpack, and decide to make brownies for Tory.

I'm taking them out of the oven when she comes through the courtyard from the office. "I smell chocolate."

I cut her a slice of warm gooeyness.

"Ohmigawd. These are the best brownies I've ever had in my entire life."

"I know, right? Wait." I open a bottle of Cabernet Sauvignon and pour us each a glass. "Red wine and chocolate are my favorite together."

She digs another brownie out of the pan and plops it on a plate. She puts a forkful in her mouth and takes a drink of wine, her eyes rolling back in culinary ecstasy. "Why have you never made these before? Have you been holding out on me?"

"It's a new recipe," I say, smiling.

"What's with the dreamy look?"

"It's the Crawford family's secret brownie recipe."

"And how did you get that?"

"I was lying in a hammock, scrolling through social media, and I saw a photo of Ashlyn Roberts—I mean, Crawford—saying she was in Cabo. I texted her and asked if she wanted to do lunch the next day. We agreed on a location. But when I got there the whole family was there."

"Was it awkward?"

"A little at first. Cade didn't look happy to see me. But then he never does."

"Then what happened?" she asks, putting her elbows on the island and making herself comfortable on a bar stool.

"No one else looked surprised to see me and insisted I join them. After quite a few margaritas, his mom invited me back to their house to make brownies. She was teaching Ashlyn the secret family recipe and said she'd teach me, too."

"So you made brownies."

"Well, the walk back was hot, so we went swimming first."

"And was Cade shirtless for that?" she asks with a smirk.

"Of course, he was."

"Which bikini were you wearing?"

"The peach crocheted one."

"Did he like it? Stop making me ask questions. Did anything happen? Did you kiss? Make wonderful love on the beach under the stars? Are you back together? Getting married? Having babies?"

"Um, no. We kind of flirted in the pool. He licked brownie batter off my finger. Walked me home." I stop and take a deep breath. "I apologized, Tory."

Her eyes get big. "You did? I'm so proud of you. Then did you kiss?"

"No. We were outside my hotel. I touched his scar, told him I was sorry, then pretty much ran into the lobby."

Tory narrows her eyes at me. "Why didn't you invite him up? Have years-in-the-making-make-up sex?"

"Because."

"Because is not an answer."

A text pops up on my phone, which is sitting on the counter.

"His ears must be burning," she says, grabbing it. "Cade wants to know if he can ask you a question. I'm going to reply yes, because I think his question is going to be something like, *Will you come over and let me put my P in your V?*"

"Tory! Give me my phone!" I rip it out of her hand and look at his message.

**Cade:** *Can I ask you a question?*

I reply.

**Me:** *Yes.*

While we wait for him to text back, she says, "You should invite him over for brownies and then, like, cover yourself in batter."

"Do you think that would work?"

"Hell, I'd lick this batter off you myself. I need the recipe. I'm seeing this new guy again tonight. We met while you were out of town."

"How old is he?"

"Twenty-four, not that it matters. What matters is he has abs so perfect they look photo shopped, and he fucks like a champ."

I can't help but laugh at Tory. "I wish I could be more laid back about sex."

"That's the problem with you. You can't separate casual sex from relationship sex. They are two different animals completely—and this new guy is an animal." She curls her fingers and makes a scratching motion. "I mean, rawr!"

I take another sip of my wine, staring at my phone and willing him to reply. When my phone vibrates, I hold it to my chest to read it. I don't want Tory to see it before I do.

**Cade:** *When you said I'm sorry, what did you mean?*

I grab my wine, take a gulp, and let out gush of air, trying to calm myself.

"What did he say?" she asks.

"Um," I reply, tears filling my eyes.

"Did he say something bad?" She snatches my phone, reads the text, then hands it back to me. "So you apologized, but he doesn't know what you apologized for?"

I cover my face with my hands and take another calming breath. My heart is racing, like it does every time I talk to him. "You can take the rest of the afternoon off," I tell her.

"Are you really going all boss on me?"

"You can take the brownies with you," I offer, trying to appease her, but needing her to leave. I need to be alone for this.

She pretends to be put off, but grabs the pan and her purse. "I'm out. See you tomorrow, *boss*."

I clutch my phone to my chest and wait for her to leave, before going to sit outside. I take in my view of the Hollywood Hills and contemplate what I meant.

**Me:** *I was apologizing for giving you the scar. For throwing a curling iron at you. What if I would have hit your eye or something?*
**Cade:** *Oh, okay.*

I can feel the disappointment in his reply.

**Me:** *Honestly, Cade, I've owed you an apology for a long time. Not just for the curling iron, but for everything.*

**Cade:** *It's nice to feel like you don't hate me anymore.*

**Me:** *I never hated you.*

**Cade:** *Sorry to cut our conversation short, but I have to step into a meeting. I was just thinking about you. About us. About what you said. It got me wondering. Take care, Palmer.*

I cover my mouth with my hand, fighting back the tears. All my emotions from this week mix with the ones from the past. The regret, the sadness, and the pain still feeling way too fresh.

But mostly it's the way he ended the conversation. *Take care, Palmer* sounds like goodbye forever. And even though I've managed fine without him, I think I always held a flicker of hope.

I break down and cry, knowing that hope was just extinguished.

# October 28th
## Cade

I'M AT AN industry event talking business with one of my biggest clients, actress Keatyn Douglas, who is just back from her honeymoon.

"So, are you and Aiden really going to live full-time in Sonoma, making wine and babies?"

"Yes, we are. What about you? Isn't it time you settle down? I always thought you'd marry Palmer."

"I did, too," I mutter.

"Cade, don't let life get in the way of your happiness. Do you know what I'm saying?"

"Our love is all that matters?" I tease, reciting a line from the movie trilogy based on her life.

"Exactly. Speaking of love," she says, glancing down at her phone. "Aiden says he managed to snag a table at the bar. What do you say we go watch the game?"

"That sounds good. So, how's married life?" I ask as we exit the hotel ballroom.

"Amazing." My phone buzzes, prompting her to say, "I think you're ringing."

I pull my phone out.

"It's Carter. Hang on." I answer the phone. "Hey, what's up?" I say to my brother.

"Are you watching the game?" he asks.

"Keatyn and I were just heading down to the bar to catch some of it. Are you there? Who's winning?"

"Yeah, I'm at the game. Cade, Pike just got hurt. It's bad."

I rush to the bar.

People are gathered around the television screens, and I hear an announcer say, *Due to the graphic nature of the injury, we aren't able to replay it.*

"What happened?" I ask Aiden, whose table I sit down at, and Carter who is still on the phone.

Aiden shoves his phone in front of me and plays me a video of the accident.

It *is* graphic.

Pike was pitching. A ground ball is hit to the first baseman. Pike leaves the pitcher's mound to make the play at first. The batter steps on his outstretched leg as they are both racing for the bag.

I wince upon seeing the ankle bend in a way that it's not supposed to and then break.

"Oh, shit. That's not good," I say aloud. "Has to be heartbreaking for him. It's his first World Series."

"I'm more concerned about his life," Carter says in my ear. "They are still out on the field trying to get him stabilized."

"Stabilized? Why?"

"It's an open compound fracture, and the bone is protruding through the skin. There's blood loss, and he's gone into shock, but that's not why I called. Palmer was in the same box with me. She's freaking out. Said she couldn't watch. She's out in the hallway. The medics surrounded him, but we're on the first baseline and could see very clearly what happened."

"Will you drive her to the hospital, Carter? Please. I don't want her driving herself."

"Of course, I will."

I hear him say, "This is for you."

Then Palmer says, "Hello?" into his phone.

"It's gonna be okay, Palmer," I tell her, trying to convey a soothing quality to my voice and not the hyped up way I feel.

"Cade?" She starts sobbing, like she's been holding it all in. "He's done playing, isn't he?"

"I don't know, Rookie," I say, calling her the nickname I used when she was little. I haven't called her that in years and have no idea why it slipped out.

"It all happened so quickly. He made a beautiful play, and the next thing you know he's on the ground writhing in pain. You could see his bone sticking out of his leg and there was blood. How does that happen?"

"The batter's foot landed on Pike's leg down by his

ankle as they were both going for the base. They'll probably have to do surgery, but he'll be fine. I want you to let Carter drive you to the hospital. Promise me."

"I promise, Cade," she says before ending the call.

I text my brother immediately.

**Me:** *I'm coming to the hospital. Her mom lives in Palm Springs, so she'll be alone. Tell me where they take him. And don't leave her until I get there.*

"It sounds pretty bad," Aiden says. "I was listening to a live feed. It's hard to hear what they're saying in the noisy bar, but they speculate a broken ankle. Which isn't really speculation since you can see the bone protruding in the video."

"I don't know how you can keep watching that," Keatyn says. "And I'm tired. Aiden, would you mind heading home now?"

Aiden grins at his new wife, his love apparent. "Not in the least, Mrs. Arrington."

We say our goodbyes.

I call my driver and have him pick me up.

"I don't know where we're going, so just park for now," I tell him. Then I search the Internet for any news I can find. I watch the play repeatedly, but my mind is seeing a different accident.

*Pike is on fire. He throws two beautiful fastballs straight down the middle to me.*

*Strike one.*

*Strike two.*

*I give him the signal for the third pitch. It's the bottom of the ninth. Bases loaded. One out. We are up by two in the final game of the College World Series. The guy hasn't swung at a pitch yet, so I call for another fastball. All we need is one strike, and then we're only one more out from a national championship.*

*Pike winds up, throws another screaming fast pitch.*

*The batter swings.*

*Connects.*

*Pop fly to centerfield.*

*The ball is caught.*

*We now have two outs.*

*One more and the game is over.*

*I take position over home plate, watching the runner advance toward me as the throw from center comes in. It's low, so I crouch down to catch it, then turn to tag the runner, who immediately barrels into me, knocking me back into a somersault. I hear a pop, feel pain instantly radiating up my leg.*

*I cover my head with my hands and roll on the ground.*

*Pike is next to me, holding my shoulder, while the trainers determine that I wasn't hit in the head but injured my leg. I get helped off the field and into the dugout.*

*Pike follows. "They called him safe. The winning run's on second. You're my catcher. What should I do?"*

*"Just throw three more strikes, dude. Three more fast-*

*balls, that's all we need. It's our year."*

*"It's our year," he says, walking back to the mound.*

*"Let's get you to the clubhouse," the trainer says to me.*

*"No, I need to stay here. Pike's going to throw three more strikes. We're going to win."*

*"He's their best batter, Cade. It doesn't look good."*

*"I've worked for this all year, and I'm going to be here when we win. Can't you just throw a boot on it or something?"*

*"I thought you said it was broken?"*

*"It is. I heard it pop. Doesn't matter right now, though. You're about to witness history in the making."*

*He sits me down and carefully takes off my shoe. The team physician joins us in the dugout, feels my leg, says, "This might hurt a little," and then sets the break, gently puts it in a boot, and then clamps it shut. "Don't put any weight on it until we can get it X-rayed," he says as Pike winds up and throws.*

*Strike one. The guy doesn't even take a swing.*

*My replacement throws the ball back to him.*

*He winds up again.*

*The guy swings hard. Completely misses.*

*Strike two.*

*The girls in the stands are yelling and holding out their I Got Piked shirts—many of whom I've 'piked' myself. One of the benefits of being part of an unstoppable duo on the field.*

*The crowd is roaring and rocking the bleachers.*

*They can feel it, history about to be made for our school.*
*I cheer as loudly as I can.*

*Pike looks at the catcher, shakes his head. He doesn't like*
*the signal. The replacement gives him another signal. Pike*
*shakes his head again. Finally, he calls for an inside strike.*

*Pike doesn't hesitate. Just throws a rocket directly above*
*the player's knees. The batter swings wildly and misses!*

*Strike three!*

*Holy shit! We win!*

*The team rushes the mound, everyone jumping on top of*
*Pike and ending up in a pile on the dirt.*

*I can't run out and celebrate with the team, so I just*
*stand here, clapping.*

*It is the greatest moment in my life up until this point.*

*Even greater than when both Pike and I were picked in*
*the first round of the major league draft a few weeks earlier.*

I didn't know it at the time, but that injury would
end my baseball career.

My phone beeps with a text, giving me the name of
the hospital, and brings me back to the present.

**Carter:** Pike will be pissed if he finds out you are at
the hospital.

**Me:** I don't give a fuck anymore. It's partially his fault
we broke up.

**Carter:** What do you mean? I thought you and Palmer
broke up over a business deal.

**Me:** Over a nudity clause. When Pike asked me to take

*her on as a client, he made me promise that I wouldn't let her do that. And before their dad died, he said pretty much the same. That's why I was so adamant about it.*

**Carter:** *So you weren't just being a jealous prick?*

**Me:** *No.*

**Carter:** *So you fucked up your relationship with her in order to not fuck up your relationship with her brother, but in the end fucked them both up?*

**Me:** *Pretty much.*

**Carter:** *Sucks. You need to fix it.*

**Me:** *Can't. Pike hates me. He doesn't forgive. Or forget.*

**Carter:** *Fuck him, bro. I mean you need to fix it with Palmer. After all, you caught the garter. You're destined to be the next at the altar.*

**Me:** *Screw you.*

When I get to the hospital, Carter comes down to get me. Apparently, Pike's location in the hospital is being kept a secret. No surprise, really. I'm sure the media is hounding the hospital for information in every way they can think of.

"Cade," Palmer says as my brother sits next to her and wraps his arm around her. I want to kill him, but she leans into it, apparently needing the comfort. "You didn't need to come."

"I have a meeting I can't get out of," Carter says, giving her another squeeze before getting up. "Cade is going to stay with you."

Maybe I won't have to kill him.

A few minutes after he leaves, a man dressed in scrubs comes out. "Palmer Montlake?"

"Yes."

"I'm Doctor Swann, the team's surgeon. Pike is stable, has been given antibiotics, and is now being prepped for surgery. He's got an open compound fracture of the tibia that we'll reposition to its normal alignment using screws and a metal plate. The fibula is fractured, as well, and we expect to find a lot of ligament damage that we'll address. He'll spend a night in the hospital then should be good to go home."

"Is he going to be able to play again?"

"It's really hard for me to say at this point, but the damage is pretty severe."

"Take good care of him," Palmer begs.

The doctor smiles at her. "You can be sure we will."

As soon as he leaves the room, she throws her hands over her face and cries, "It's all my fault, Cade. I jinxed him."

"What do you mean?"

"Last year I wished him good luck before the playoff games, and he lost. So this year, he made me wait until the World Series. And he didn't want me to wish him luck. So, I told him to break a leg. And he did!"

I wrap my arm around her and pat her back. "It's not

your fault, Palmer. Really, it's not. It was a freak accident. He'll be fine."

A big-chested knockout in high heels teeters into the room. "Palmer! How is he? All the reporters are saying it's going to be the end of his career!"

"Hey, Bethany. I'm not sure. He's going into surgery. I'm surprised they let you up here. It's supposed to be family only."

"I'm *practically* family," she says, showing off a diamond almost as big as a baseball on her right hand. "See what Pike gave me for luck? As soon as he wins the World Series, I'm pretty sure he's going to propose!"

"That's great," Palmer says flatly, clearly annoyed by her presence.

"Bethany, I'm Cade." I hold out my hand. "Why don't we go get some coffees?"

After we walk down the hall for a bit, she pulls a flask out of her purse. "Coffee is a great idea. I need something to put this in. I'm so stressed! What if he can never play again?"

"I'm just hoping he can walk again. That's what you should be worried about."

"What? Like he could be paralyzed?"

Pike never did date the smart ones. "Um, *no.* That only happens when you injure your *spine.* The ankle joint allows us to walk properly. It's probably going to take a while before his will work again."

"Do you think they'll still let me go on the field if the team wins the World Series? Will I get to go to all the parties? Be interviewed?"

"I don't know. Did he give you the special passes?"

"No! Shit! All this work to get here, and he has to get himself hurt. I have the worst luck."

I want to go off on this woman, but I don't. I don't want to upset Palmer any more. I point Bethany in the direction of the coffee shop in hopes that she won't be able to find her way back.

"WHERE IS BETHANY?" Palmer asks when I return to the waiting room and take a seat next to her.

"I take it you don't like her?"

"She only dates baseball players, and she's traded up to him. Pike's always been dumb when it comes to women."

"I know," I say, recalling several times in college when he got into trouble because of a girl, and even when he went on to the pros, I often had to bail him out of some kind of mess. He told me it was a good thing I was going to law school. He had a reputation for going through women faster than he went through bats. "I sent her on a coffee mission in hopes that she wouldn't find her way back." I chuckle.

Palmer's face breaks out in a smile and, for the first time since I got here, she laughs. "That is why I love you."

I suck in a big breath of air. I've longed to hear those words.

Just not in this way.

"Oh," she says, awkwardly. "You know what I mean. You always took care of me. I appreciated it then, and I appreciate it now. Pike would appreciate it, too."

"No, he wouldn't. He'd be mad."

"Don't be so sure. I remember him sitting by your side at a hospital in Omaha after *you* got hurt when he could have been out partying with the team."

"That was a long time ago."

"Still. A friendship like that should have been life-long. And would have been, if it weren't for me. I'm sorry I screwed everything up for all of us, and I'm really sorry it's taken me so long to apologize. Do you think we could ever be friends again?"

I take her hand and pat it gently. "I think we already are, Palmer."

"They actually had a Starbucks on site!" Bethany's voice booms through our quiet moment. "Thank God! I needed a green tea Frappuccino to soothe my nerves." She takes a drink from a cardboard tray and hands it to Palmer. "I wasn't sure what you liked, so I went with a skinny caramel macchiato."

"That's my favorite, Bethany," Palmer lies. Her fa-vorite has always been a non-fat peppermint mocha with whip.

"And for you," Bethany says to me. "I ordered the barista's favorite. Some sort of a peppermint concoction. He said it reminds him of when he drank peppermint schnapps and hot chocolate growing up in, like, Minnesota? Whatever that is." She hands it to me. "So, is there any news? Do we know how long we're going to have to be here? And what should I tell the press if they want to speak to me?"

I set my drink on the table next to Palmer's. A few seconds later, while Bethany is busy asking a million questions, I pick up the caramel macchiato, switching drinks with her. Palmer smiles at me and mouths *thank you.*

"You know what, Bethany?" I say. "I think I would let the team's PR handle any questions. You shouldn't have to deal with that."

She sits up straighter. "You're right. I shouldn't have to deal with such pettiness. I'm just so stressed by all of this. It ruins everything."

"I hate to see *you* stressed," Palmer says, "but imagine how my brother feels. He was playing in the biggest game of his life."

"That's exactly my point! I had to buy a whole new wardrobe to wear to all the events, for traveling, and for the games. Now, I don't know if I'll get to wear them all!"

Palmer rolls her eyes.

"You know what, Bethany? Why don't I get my driver to take you back to your hotel, so you can get some rest. I'm going to send Palmer home soon, too. There really isn't anything either of you can do while he's in surgery. Go get some sleep and come back here in the morning when he's awake."

"That's a great idea," she says, checking her phone. "The team is back at the hotel now. I could join them for a quick nightcap and then get some sleep."

"Exactly," I agree. I call my driver and escort her out of the hospital.

WHEN I GET back to the waiting room, Palmer is pacing and watching the clock.

"Shouldn't we have heard something by now?"

"It's only been about an hour, Palmer."

"Really? It seems like it's been forever." She yawns.

"Come sit down." I get her situated on a couch next to me, wrap my arm around her, and let her rest her head on my shoulder.

"I'm going to fall asleep if I lean on you like this."

"That's okay. I'll wake you when the doctor comes out."

HOURS LATER, WE'RE both woken by a nurse.

"He's doing fine and is in recovery. The doctor will

be out to see you shortly."

Another hour later, we're taken into a small room to meet with the surgeon.

"How is he?" Palmer asks, tightly squeezing my hand.

"He tolerated surgery well." He puts an X-ray up onto a lighted board. "You can see here that the fibula protruded through the skin." He points to another area. "The tibia is fractured, here. The ankle dislocated. The talus, which is this here at the top of the foot, is cracked." He puts another X-ray up next to it. "This is after surgery. We inserted nineteen pins and screws and repaired the soft tissue."

"How long will he be in the hospital?" I ask.

"I expect we'll discharge him later today or tomorrow. He'll be in a wheelchair, as we won't want any weight on it for quite a while. I know he sold his home in L.A. when he moved to Tampa. Does he have somewhere he can recuperate locally, or would you like me to recommend a rehabilitation facility?"

"He can stay at my house. It's one level and has wide doorways."

"Perfect." He gives us a room number. "You're welcome to go there now and wait for him. He should be coming out of recovery shortly."

I escort Palmer to the assigned room.

"The surgeon didn't tell us much about his recovery

time," she says.

"He'll talk to Pike about that." I take her hand in mine. "Look, I don't think I should be here when Pike gets to the room. I wouldn't want to upset him. I'll stay in the waiting room."

"Oh, Cade. You've done enough. You can go now. Really, I'm fine."

"Are you sure?"

"Yeah, he's out of surgery and doing well. I just want to be here when he wakes up."

"You call me if you need anything, okay? Even if it's just for a non-fat peppermint mocha with whip."

She puts her palm across her chest. "You remember that?"

"I remember everything, Palmer. Goodnight."

# October 29th
## Palmer

PIKE IS WHEELED into his hospital room and situated on the bed.

"Hey," I say, running my hand across his forehead. "How are you feeling?"

"Tired," he says, floating off to sleep.

I sink into the recliner next to the bed and close my eyes.

I'M AWAKENED BY my phone ringing.

I quickly hit mute, not wanting to wake Pike, and go out into the hall to answer it.

"Palmer! Oh my gosh! Your mother just called me freaking out. How is Pike? How are you? Where are you? What do you need?"

"Slow down, Tory," I say. "Pike is fine."

"Why didn't you call me last night when it happened? You shouldn't have been alone."

"I wasn't alone. Carter Crawford was in the same skybox as I was. He drove me to the hospital. Cade met us here and stayed with me all through the surgery."

"Oh, he did, did he?"

"Don't even start. He was just being nice."

"So what can I do?"

"Pike will need to recuperate at my house. So get the guest room ready and order in a bunch of food. Guy food. He usually eats pretty healthy, but with him sitting around, he'll want snacks—the not so healthy kind. And clear my schedule for a few days. I want to be there with him. I'll call my mother right now."

"I'm on it," she says and hangs up.

I walk back into the room to find Pike sitting up, awake.

"How are you doing? I was just about to call Mom. I totally forgot to call her last night."

"She probably fell asleep watching the game. She would have called you otherwise. And I'm starving."

"Hit the button beside your bed and page the nurse. I'll call Mom."

I dial her number.

"Hey, Mom."

"Palmer Alexis Montlake, I can't believe you didn't call me last night! I shouldn't have to find out about my son's injury from ESPN."

"Things were a little hectic last night, and I didn't want to wake you. I'm giving you to Pike, now," I say, handing him the phone.

"Hey, Mom. I know. I know. Yeah, I'm going to be fine. Just a broken ankle. No, you don't need to come." He hands me the phone back. "She wants to talk to you."

I take the phone and give my mom every single detail she demands before she'll let me go.

"Where's Bethany?" Pike asks me after I hang up.

"She went back to the hotel while you were in surgery last night—said she needed a drink. I texted her when you were out of surgery and let her know your room number. I'm sure she'll be here this morning."

"I can't even believe this happened. I come back better than ever from shoulder surgery, make it through the playoffs, and am in the first game of the World Series."

"I'm sorry, Pike. It sucks."

"Yeah, it does."

"I was worried about you," I admit. "It was a bad break."

"I saw it. Passed out. Don't remember a whole lot until I was in the ambulance."

"It's probably better that way."

He grins at me. "Is there a video of it?"

# *Pike*

I SEND MY sister home to get some sleep, telling her I don't want her to come back until later tonight. She looks exhausted.

I'm tired too, but don't get much rest.

Most of my teammates and coaches stop by to see me, as does the opposing team's player who feels horrible that he stepped on my ankle.

Bethany doesn't show up until late in the afternoon, bringing me just the pants portion of the sweat-suit I asked for. She's dressed to kill, but I can tell she's hung over, based on the recovery drink she's carefully sipping on. She asks a million questions about when I'll be able to play again and about her attending the rest of the games and events.

Not once does she really ask about me.

She stays for a very short time then tells me she needs to get to the game to *represent me*, gives me a kiss, and leaves.

A delivery service drops off the personal effects from my locker, and for the first time since last night, I'm able to check my phone. There are so many social media notifications from fans everywhere that I have to turn them all off. There are hundreds of texts from my teammates, my former teammates, news reporters, and friends. I quickly scroll through them, not responding, until one catches my eye.

**Cameron:** *I know it's been a while since we've talked, but I wanted you to know I'm thinking of you. If you need anything. Anything at all. You call me. I mean it, Pike. Just because we aren't together, doesn't mean I don't still care for you.*

A reporter asked me early in my career if I had a celebrity crush. I answered truthfully that it was Cameron Barella. I had just seen the movie where she played an FBI agent who infiltrated a group of surfers who were robbing banks, and she was the first actress who'd popped into my head. Not surprising, though. She was in a bikini for most of the movie. She's an exotic beauty, with a curvy figure, long dark hair, lush lips, and gorgeous, almond-shaped eyes.

A few months later, I was visiting a children's hospital with a few other celebrities, one of whom was Cameron. When I passed her in the hall, she said, *I hear you're hot for me, bat boy.*

*You got that right,* I had replied, cocky as ever. *Drinks after?*

She shrugged. *Sure, why not?*

It was the start of something beautiful, and we quickly fell in love. But the realities of our careers and crazy schedules meant we were apart more than we were together. But when we were together, things were magical. Incredible sex. A lot of laughter. Cameron was the girl I wanted to settle down with, but she didn't want to settle down. She loved her career as much as I loved mine. Our time apart took its toll, and we broke up. We've tried numerous times over the last ten years to make it work. It just never does.

> **Me:** *That means a lot, Cam. Thank you. Palmer said she had lunch with you in Milan. You still there?*
> **Cameron:** *No, I just finished a location shoot in Morocco. I'm in London for a few weeks then headed back home.*
> **Me:** *Drinks after?*
> **Cameron:** *Oh my gosh, Pike. You were such a cocky shit back then. Of course, I want drinks after, Pike. I always have.*

I look down at my leg. I've been feeling pretty depressed since the doctor came in this morning and told me that the bone would heal just fine, but that there was so much cartilage damage it will require significant rehab just to walk again.

At some point, I'm going to have to figure my life out—just not today.

"YOU'RE BEING RELEASED," a chipper nurse tells me. "Your sister is on her way to pick you up."

A few minutes later, I'm being carefully loaded into an Escalade limousine. Neon lights flash across the ceiling. As the driver pulls away from the hospital, my sister looks around and starts laughing.

"I think I overestimated the length of your leg," she says.

"I bet not many people are picked up from the hospital in a stretch limo. Where's the party?" I joke, but it comes off flat. The truth is, for once in my life, I'm in no mood to party. I'm pissed. Mad at the world. Mad at myself. Mad at my foot. I should be at the stadium right now, warming up in the bullpen, pumping the team up for Game Two.

AS PALMER IS getting me set up in front of the television in her family room, Tory shows up with bags full of take out.

"I wasn't sure what you'd be in the mood for, so I just bought it all," she says, setting out hot wings, sushi, burgers, onion rings, and barbecue sandwiches.

"It all looks amazing," I tell her, starting with the hot wings. "Thank you."

"I heard you had a lot of visitors today," Palmer says. "You need your rest."

"You sure you're okay with putting me up?" I ask.

"Of course, I am."

"And Bethany too?"

"Absolutely," Palmer says, but I know she doesn't care for her. And honestly, I probably shouldn't either. It's pretty obvious that she's more in love with my being a ball player than she is with me.

We flip on the game, chow down, and watch as my team loses without me.

# October 30th
## *Palmer*

I'M MAKING LUNCH while Tory sits at the kitchen island, going over my calendar with me.

"So have you talked to Cade since the hospital?" she whispers.

"We've texted a bit. Nothing earth shattering. He mostly keeps checking in with me, asking if there's anything I need."

"What did you say to that?" she asks, her eyes getting strangely large.

I shrug as I throw cut-up veggies into a wok on the stove. "I don't remember. That you were taking care of getting the house ready, probably."

"For future reference, Palmer, when a man that scrumptious asks you if there's anything you need, your response should be: *What I need is your cock in me. Now.*"

"Tory!" I scream-laugh. "You're so bad. I could never say that."

"Sure you could. Promise me. Next time someone asks you that, it will be your response."

I roll my eyes at her while I add cooked chicken and some teriyaki sauce to the stir fry.

"Okay, back to business," Tory says, reading from her list. "I'll let the grocery service know that you won't be in Tahoe this weekend, and I've already sent your regrets for the two industry events next week. We are rescheduling Kimmel and the magazine interview for later this month."

"Why are you rescheduling everything?" Pike asks, wheeling himself into the kitchen.

"Because I need to take care of you," I reply.

"I'm not a child, Palmer. I can take care of myself while you're gone. I just needed somewhere to stay. I don't need a nurse."

"I won't be able to focus on that stuff, knowing you're home by yourself."

Pike's phone buzzes. "Bethany is just pulling up. I won't be alone."

I turn the gas down and throw a lid over the stir fry.

"OH, BABYCAKES!" BETHANY yells. I swear, when she's around the sound level goes up two decibels. "You're in a wheelchair! Will you ever be able to walk again?"

"I'm not paralyzed, Bethany. I just can't put weight on it. It's in a splint until the wound heals. Once that happens, they can put a cast on it, and I'll be able to use crutches to get around."

"What wound?" she asks.

Pike closes his eyes and takes a calming breath. You can tell his blood pressure has shot up in the few minutes she's been here. "If you would have been at the hospital with me, instead of at the game last night, you'd know the answer to that question," he huffs.

She drapes herself all over him. "Babycakes, I told you that I felt like one of us needed to be at the game. I had to go. Can you help me with this luggage?" She drops it in the entryway for him and wanders through the house.

"Your house isn't as grand as I thought it would be, Palmer," she says, as Tory and I grab the bags. "I guess it will have to do. The team left to go back to Florida this morning, so I got kicked out of my hotel room."

Tory gives the girl a glare.

Tory would scare me, but I don't think Bethany even catches on to the fact that in the three seconds she's been here, she's slammed my house, asked my wheelchair bound brother to fetch her bags, and complained about not being able to leave with the team.

Bethany goes through the kitchen and looks out the French doors to the backyard. "Well, at least you have a pool. What do you say, Pike, let's go for a swim."

"What part of *he just broke three bones in his ankle and had surgery less than forty-eight hours ago and has numerous stitches* don't you understand?" I ask the little bitch.

"Well, you don't need to get all huffy about it. Pike likes to see me in a bikini. If he can't swim, he can watch. Just because he's not valid, doesn't mean he has to sit inside all day."

"Not valid?" Pike asks, confused.

"I think she means *invalid*," Tory says, stifling a laugh.

"Same diff," Bethany says, waving her off. "I'm going to put on my bikini."

"Your suitcase is pretty small," I say to my brother. "What's in here?"

"Two suits to wear and some workout clothes. Not much."

"We're going to need to get you some things," Tory says. "What size are you?"

"Usually just a large. Like for workout shorts and T-shirts. That's all I'll need for a while. It's not like I'm going anywhere anytime soon."

Tory gives me a pointed look, telling me that she'll be coming back with a full wardrobe and it will *not* include just shorts and T-shirts.

"And I'm serious," Pike says, "about you not cancelling your plans."

"Would you want to come up to Tahoe with me?"

"What were you going for?"

"I have some scripts to read for my production company. Thought it would be nice to go up there. I haven't been since this summer."

Pike shakes his head. "No, you go. It might be good for Bethany and I to have some alone time to discuss things."

"Like what?"

"I think her idea of my future and the reality of my future aren't quite in sync."

Bethany comes out of the bedroom wearing a leopard bikini with a thong bottom and a triangle top so small it barely covers her nipples. She grabs Pike's wheelchair and pushes him out to the courtyard.

"That woman is about as subtle as a wrecking ball," Tory says, shaking her head. "So what do you want me to do about your schedule?"

I dish up the stir fry. "Let's not cancel Tahoe just yet. Leave the rest."

She looks out at the courtyard, where Bethany is rubbing her thong against Pike, and shakes her head. "I think that's probably a wise decision."

# October 31st
## Pike

"BABYCAKES," BETHANY SAYS, waking me from my nap by tugging on my dick.

"Um, I'm supposed to stay immobile for a bit."

"So that's how it's going to be?" she smarts.

"For a few more days, yes. The doctor is coming by this afternoon to check on me. We'll see what he says."

"It's not like your dick's broken," she mutters. "Are you depressed? When I was at the bar with the team after the game, Craig told me that I should watch you for depression. That athletes often have a hard time dealing with an injury. I told him you'd be back at it in no time. He said you'll never play again. Is that true?"

"It's really too soon to tell," I mutter, wanting to go kick Craig's ass for even daring to say that out loud. Of course, out of all the guys on the team, she'd have to listen to the one who is the biggest prick.

The doorbell rings.

I glance at the clock. "That's probably the doctor," I say. "Go get dressed."

A few minutes later, Palmer brings the doctor to the bedroom.

"How are we feeling?" he asks. "Are you getting plenty of rest?"

"I just woke up from a nap, so yes."

"Let's unwrap it and take a look. We're most concerned about infection at this point, so you need to watch for that. Any sign of redness, increased swelling, or increased pain. Anything unusual, you call me right away."

"When can I get out of the wheelchair?"

"I figured you'd ask that. Not until the wound heals, which will take a week or two."

Bethany comes out of the bathroom fully dressed and made up.

"When will he be able to play baseball again?" she asks, plopping onto the bed and sending a wave of pain through my leg.

"Everyone heals differently, so I can't answer that question. He'll be able to return to normal activities once the bones are fully healed. Then he'll need some physical therapy to regain full movement and strength. It could take up to a year to regain full ankle function."

"A year?!" Bethany exclaims. "That's unacceptable."

"I'm afraid that's not for you to determine, Miss," the doctor says.

"Will he play baseball again?" she asks in desperation.

He studies my face then turns to her. "*That* is up to him."

AFTER THE DOCTOR leaves, Bethany announces that she's going shopping.

"With my credit card?" I ask.

"Of course, with your credit card, Pike. It's your fault I'm stuck here."

## Cade

"YOUR FATHER IS on line two," my assistant says from the intercom on my phone.

"Hey, Dad."

"Do you have any plans for Halloween tonight, Cade?"

"Not specifically, why?"

He lets out a huge breath. "Well, thank goodness. Could you please come over and hand out candy here?"

"Uh, sure. Why?"

"Your mother and I have a retirement party for a very dear friend of mine, and she won't go if no one is here to hand out candy. She says it's a tradition. And that woman is stubborn. It was fine until Chloe just informed us she won't be home. Your brother is out of town, and

Ashlyn and Cash have plans. You're my last hope, son."

"Sure, Dad. I'll do it."

"I'm rewriting my will as we speak, and you're getting everything." Dad chuckles. "Actually, your mother says there will be chili and cornbread in the warming drawer for you."

"That sounds great. See you soon."

I hang up, press the intercom, and say to my assistant, "Can you cancel drinks tonight? I have a family thing."

"Sure thing, boss," she replies.

I PUSH THE contract I was going over to the side of my desk.

I can't stop thinking about Palmer.

I'm glad we're friends again, but I want us to be more.

I decide to go with the friendly route.

**Me:** *Happy Halloween.*
**Palmer:** *You too. You trick or treating tonight?*
**Me:** *No, going to my parents to hand out candy. They have some event, and Mom was freaking out that no one would be there to answer the door. Carter is in Tampa for Game Three, Chloe has some party, and Cash and Ashlyn had plans, too.*
**Palmer:** *That sounds fun.*
**Me:** *Would you want to join me?*
**Palmer:** *I can't really leave Pike.*

**Me:** *I thought you said Bethany was there.*

**Palmer:** *If Bethany had her way, she'd have him swinging naked from my chandelier.*

**Me:** *Now that sounds like a party.*

**Palmer:** *Ugh.*

**Me:** *It's probably hard having both of them in your house.*

**Palmer:** *Pike's fine. She's driving me nuts.*

**Me:** *All the more reason to get out.*

**Palmer:** *Good point. I'll be there.*

# Pike

I'M SITTING OUTSIDE near the pool, trying to pretend I'm on vacation and not stuck here. It's only been a few days, but I feel like the walls are closing in on me. I'm not where I'm supposed to be. I'm pissed at myself for getting hurt. I'm pissed at Bethany's shitty attitude and the fact that she's out shopping.

I'm pissed at the fucking world.

My phone buzzes with a text.

**Cameron:** *How's the invalid?*

**Me:** *Pretty shitty, honestly.*

**Cameron:** *I suppose being stuck in a wheelchair is driving you nuts. You're used to always being on the go.*

**Me:** *I'm going crazy.*

**Cameron:** *What did the doctor say about going out?*

**Me:** *It will be easier to go out once I have a cast.*

**Cameron:** *When I get back, let's do drinks. You can even bring the girlfriend. I promise I'll play nice.*

**Me:** *It's a date then.*

My phone buzzes again. I expect it to be from Cameron, but it's from my catcher and good buddy, Rob.

**Rob:** *I hate to tell you this while you're recouping, but that girl you've been seeing. . .*

**Me:** *What about her?*

**Rob:** *I've been trying to decide if I should tell you or not, after everything that's happened to you. But I think you should know. Just don't kill the messenger, okay?*

**Me:** *Who did she sleep with?*

**Rob:** *Craig.*

I slam my phone down in outrage. That fucking little bitch.

I immediately call the credit card company and turn off the card I gave her for travel expenses. She never uses it for that, though. She mostly racks up big bills for clothing in every city we go to.

It's a good thing I'm in this wheelchair, or I'd fucking kill her. I momentarily envision knocking her to the ground and running over her repeatedly with the wheelchair. But who am I kidding? All that would do is piss her off.

A few minutes later, I get a text from her.

**Bethany:** *Babycakes, my credit card isn't working. Can you call and fix it?*

Needless to say, I don't reply.

Instead, I go inside and stew about it for nearly two hours until she comes storming into the house.

"I had all these amazing things picked out at Neiman's, and my credit card got declined! I sent you a text and told you to fix it. But you didn't!"

"I didn't see your text," I say flatly.

"Bullshit! I called the credit card company myself, and they said my card had been cancelled! How does that even happen? You should be outraged!"

"You could have just put it on your own card, if you needed it that bad."

"I couldn't afford it."

"You're right, you can't. And I'm sick of you spending my money."

"What the fuck is going on? Is it because I went shopping instead of sitting around here and waiting on you?"

"I would think if you cared about me, that's exactly where you'd want to be. And your card got declined because *I* cancelled it."

"Why the fuck would you do that?!"

"Why the fuck would you sleep with Craig?"

Her eyes get big. "Who told you that? Whoever did is lying! I would never—"

"Save me the lies, Bethany. Pack up your shit and get the fuck out."

"Fine. I don't want to be with a fucking washed up has-been. And that's exactly what Craig says you're going to be, because your career is over!"

She storms into the bedroom, tosses shit around, and then marches out the door with her suitcase.

I WHEEL MYSELF into the kitchen to get a drink, slamming my leg into the wall on the way, which sends a shockwave of pain through my body, causing me to shudder.

"Fuck!" I yell, backing up, only to bump into a table behind me.

The table tips over, everything on it spiraling to the ground and breaking with a loud crash.

"Fuck! Fuck! Fuck! Fuck this leg. Fuck this table. And fuck my fucking life!"

## Palmer

I WALK INTO the house with a bounce in my step, carrying the candy I stopped and got on the way home from my studio meeting. I'm excited to see Cade. I know it's just handing out candy, but—

"Fuck!" I hear Pike yell out.

Then there's a loud crash and, "Fuck! Fuck! Fuck! Fuck this leg. Fuck this table. And fuck my fucking life!"

I run through the breezeway and into the kitchen, worried about him. I find him sitting in his wheelchair next to a tipped over decorative table, the vase that was on it shattered into pieces across the floor.

Pike's head is buried in his hands, and he's crying.

I put my hand to my chest, tears filling my eyes.

"Pike, are you okay?"

"No! I'm not fucking okay!" he cries. "I can't fucking move without running into something, and Bethany fucked my teammate."

"She what!?"

"She fucked my teammate, because he said I'd never play again. That I'd be a has-been."

I drop to my knees in front of him, not worrying about the glass. "Pike, you've had a long, successful career. No one will ever think of you that way, whether you play again or not."

"Why did this have to fucking happen to me? Why?"

"I don't know, Pike. But bad shit happens to people all the time. It's how you deal with it that shows the kind of man you are. And our father didn't raise you to feel sorry for yourself. He taught you to give back as much as you get."

"He'd be embarrassed to see me like this, wouldn't he?" he says, breaking down further.

"No, you're human. You were playing in the biggest game of your life. It's normal that you'd be upset. Who are you more upset with though, Bethany or your teammate?"

"My teammate is a complete asshat. One of the few guys I don't care much for, but he was still my teammate. There's supposed to be some respect there. Limits, you know? I need to get out of this fucking house. Can we go somewhere? Please?"

"Where do you want to go?"

"I don't fucking care. For a drive. Anywhere."

"Okay. Let's go."

I grab the keys for my SUV and rearrange the seats so Pike can sit in the way back and keep his leg straight out, get him loaded up, roll the windows down, and take off.

# Cade

FOR THE FIRST hour at my parents' house, I hand out candy wondering where Palmer is. Wondering why she didn't show or why she didn't call. Soon, I get sick of all the cute little costumes and cheerful smiles and just put a bowl full of candy out on the front porch and turn off the lights inside the house.

I eat my chili and cornbread in the dark and stare at my phone, willing her to call.

After another hour, I'm praying she's okay.

After the third hour, I'm just plain pissed, but when my phone rings, I answer it without even looking to see who is calling.

"Cade," a voice says—one that is not Palmer's.

I check the caller ID and see it's Marty, the studio attorney leading the contract deal I've been working on. I am not in the mood to talk to him, but fuck it.

"We can't go a penny higher," he continues.

"Marty, you know Gracie Stevens sells. She'll be gorgeous on all the movie posters, dolls, trinkets, and other merchandise you are going to bank on. She'll push it because of her popularity. She *is* your Warrior Goddess. You know you want her. Have you even seen how many followers she has on social media? Her app alone has two million subscribers a month. She can do live feeds straight from the set. Talk about free advertising to your target market. She could sell shit to teens if she told them it tasted good."

"She's a risk. A loose cannon. Partying and out of control." Which is a true statement. She's young, has too much money and freedom, but she's also an incredibly gifted actress.

"You're filming in the bum fuck desert. How much trouble can she get into there, really? She'll be the perfect modern-day Athena. And she'll bring in your target audience, Marty. Stop fucking around and pay us what she's worth." I'm being a dick. Marty and I are actually friends, but I'm taking my frustration and hurt out on him anyway.

"Are you really going to say no to the kind of money that's already on the table?"

"She's fifteen. She was nominated for a freaking Academy Award. She's a great actress. She has numerous other offers on the table but, for some reason, your script appealed to her the most. That's why we're in negotiations now, Marty. We're talking about a point off the top. If you keep dicking around with me, I'll make it two."

Marty sighs. "Fine. *One* point."

"And I want the accounting for that point crystal clear."

"You'll have the offer in the morning, Cade. What's up your butt anyway?"

"Nothing, Marty. Just sick of fucking around."

I hang up. And realize I told him the God's honest truth. I am tired of fucking around. I want Palmer and only her.

What the hell am I supposed to do now?

She totally blew me off.

Fuck it.

I make a quick decision to get the hell out of town, so I can think. Figure this all out. So, I call Cash. "Hey, I'm headed up to Tahoe tomorrow. Can you handle my clients for the weekend?"

"Of course," he says. "Anything pressing going on?"

"No, I've got everything pretty well buttoned up. Just call me if anything serious comes up, but otherwise I'll be back on Monday."

"Sounds good. By the way, Ashlyn and I are hoping we'll get invited to go skiing up there once they get some snow."

"You know you can use the new house anytime you want. I've got to finish getting it furnished, but I'm hoping to convince Mom and Dad to celebrate Christmas up there this year."

"That would be a lot of fun. Take care and have a good weekend!"

"You too, bro. Thanks."

I hang up, turn the lights back on, bring the empty candy bowl back inside, and wait for my parents to get home.

# *Palmer*

PIKE AND I drive around for hours, listening to Game Three on the radio. He seems to be in a better mood when we get home, even though his team lost again.

He thanks me for getting him out and goes to bed, while I clean up the glass, stand the table upright, and move it out of his path. Then I look around at my house more critically and rearrange all the furniture, making bigger, clearer paths so that Pike can more easily maneuver around in the wheelchair.

I drop into a chair in my room and suddenly realize I completely forgot about meeting Cade. I run back out to the garage, grab my purse, and take my phone out.

I have a couple missed calls from him and a few texts. When I call him back, it goes straight to voicemail. Shit.

I send a text.

**Me:** *I'm so so sorry, Cade. I got home and Pike was upset. It's a long story, but . . . I'm sorry.*

He doesn't reply.

# November 1st
## *Palmer*

"WHAT WOULD YOU think about going up to Tahoe with me?" I ask Pike as I'm cooking breakfast. Normally, I'm not up this early, but I heard him rolling around at four-thirty and decided to just get up. "I'm going to fly to Reno early this evening then drive over to the house."

"I'm not sure I'm up for all that travel. If I'm being honest, the car ride last night wore me out, and I'm sore."

"Then I'll cancel my flight and stay home."

"I saw that you moved furniture around. I appreciate that, Palmer. I'm sorry I was such a jerk last night."

"It's understandable. You've been through a lot in the last couple of days."

"I was thinking about Dad last night. You were right. He'd tell me to dust off my uniform and get back out there, so that's what I'm going to do."

"What do you mean?"

"I'd fly to the games in Florida if I thought I could handle the trip, but if the team comes back to L.A. for

Game Six, I want to go to the game and be with my team. So until then, I'm going to do everything the doctor says. Get my rest. Keep my leg up. Let it heal."

"So then we can just hang out and watch movies all weekend, like we used to do when we were kids."

"No, Palmer. You're going to Tahoe. I'm staying here."

"You're kicking me out of my own house?"

"Pretty much," he grins. "I'm going to sit my ass on the couch, cheer for my team, and order take out. Seriously, sis, just letting me stay here is enough. I don't expect you to change your schedule for me. And I could honestly use some time alone. To reflect. Get my shit together. I've had a lot of requests for interviews and need to figure all that out."

"I'll only agree to it if you are okay with Tory stopping in to check on you a couple times a day. And if you will text me and let me know you haven't, like, fallen and can't get up."

"Deal," he says with a laugh.

"Question for you," I say. "When Bethany left here, where was she going?"

"Back home, I assume."

"To *your* home? What about your stuff, Pike?"

"She wouldn't, would she?"

I stare at him. "Cash, jewelry, watches, your National Championship ring?"

His eyes get huge, and he slams his hand on the kitchen table. "Shit. Grab me my phone, will you?"

I wait while he makes some calls. When he's done, he says, "I don't know where the hell everyone is, but I've called the house phone, the housekeeper, my agent, and my neighbors. No one is answering."

"What about someone from the team?"

"They'll be getting ready for Game Four today. They don't need to worry about my shit."

"Is there anyone you know who is going to be in town for the game? Someone that could maybe run over there?"

"Carter Crawford," he says with a nod. "He'll be there."

"You should call him."

"Shit, you're right."

## Pike

I CALL CARTER, explain the Bethany situation, and ask if he'd have time to go to my place and get the locks changed.

"Do you think she's there now?" he asks.

"If she was able to get a flight last night, it would probably would have been the red eye, which would have had her landing at seven this morning. So I suppose she could be, since it's close to eight o'clock there."

"Give me the address. I'm at a hotel downtown. You're out on Davis Island, right?"

"Yeah, I am."

"Perfect, that means I'm close."

I give him my address and the security code.

"I'll go on one condition," Carter says.

"Anything. Just name it."

"When you're feeling better, I want you to have a drink with me—"

"Of course, I'll have a drink with you."

"—and my brother," he adds.

"Ah, fuck, man."

"Deal or no deal, Pike. The time is ticking."

I sigh. "Fine. Deal. Seriously, thank you."

"I'll call you when I get there and let you know how it goes."

"Fuck," I mutter to myself as I hang up.

"What'd he say?" Palmer asks me.

"He said he'd take care of everything."

"Aw, good. Let's eat breakfast while we wait for an update."

# *Cade*

THE CHARTER I use suggests changing our flight plan to land in Reno as opposed to the small Truckee airport I previously requested, due to high winds. We make the switch, take the flight, and I rent an SUV at the airport there.

I know the area is expecting some flurries today, but by the time I cross into Truckee, the snow is coming down hard and heavy. It's getting dark, the roads are slippery, and I find myself slowing down and taking each turn very carefully.

As I round a corner, I spot a car that has slid off the road. A gorgeous woman is standing outside the car with a phone to her ear, her collar turned up, shivering against the cold.

Palmer.

Shit.

Even though she tried to called me late Halloween night, I haven't called her back. I wasn't sure what to say, and I didn't want to hear whatever dumb excuse she had for not showing up. My plan was to come up here and figure out what to do regarding her.

Part of me wishes I could drive right by and pretend I don't see her.

But, I can't.

When I saw the woman on the side of the road, my

heart skipped a beat, recognizing her before I realized it was Palmer.

I put my flashers on, pull over, and roll down the passenger-side window. "Hey!"

"Cade, is that you?" she asks, her eyes wide with astonishment.

"Yeah, you need a lift?"

She glances at her car, then at me, like she's trying to decide which may be the lesser evil.

After a few seconds, she nods her head. "Yes, thank you. That would be great. The tow truck can't be here for at least an hour. I guess it's worse just west of here."

"You know, you shouldn't be out on roads like this all alone," I say, chewing her out a little. "You should have put on chains."

"I thought I could make it," she replies, causing my mind to tumble back in time.

*"I thought I could make it," she says. She's wearing a sundress, and the tip of her nose and her shoulders are a little pink from our day spent on the shores of Lake Tahoe. She's just fifteen, and I'll be turning twenty-one in a few days. She's going home with her family tomorrow, and then all our college buddies are coming up for a weekend party. To celebrate my finally being drinking-age legal.*

*What's not legal is the girl standing in front of me. But you'd never know it from looking at her. Palmer Montlake has been modeling. Already tall with the perfect body for hanging clothes from, she's just back from a European modeling trip.*

*And, boy, has she ever grown up. In more ways than one. Most importantly, is the fact that I'm sure she's flirting with me.*

*I know I need to make her stop.*

*But I'm a little drunk, and she's way too pretty for her own good. Not to mention the fact that she was running around in a skimpy bikini all day long. But having her cover up doesn't mean I've forgotten about how she looked.*

*I chastise myself.*

*She's just a kid. She's fifteen. Not only that, she's my best friend's kid sister—the holy grail of what you don't mess with.*

*She runs her hand down my arm, laughs, and says, "Will you put a Band-Aid on it for me?"*

*When she was trying to jump from the boat to the dock like her brother and I did, she caught her flip-flop on the edge and crashed—cutting her knee.*

*"It's not that bad," I hesitate, knowing that under no circumstances can I can allow myself to touch her. I'm afraid if I do, I won't be able to stop.*

*"Come on, Cade," she pouts, puffing out her sexy bottom lip. "I've helped you before. Remember a couple years ago when you were bleeding after sliding into home plate? I fixed you all up."*

*I remember it, alright. But she didn't look like this back then. She was gawky and awkward like a gelding, not the gorgeous gazelle she is today.*

*She jumps up onto the kitchen counter, immediately causing my mind to think about what naughty things I'd do to her on this counter if she were as old as she looks.*

*I take a deep breath, calm myself down, and put the Band-Aid gently across her knee.*

*She kisses me on the cheek in return. What should be a quick thank-you peck is long and drawn out, and her scent lingers on me.*

*"Thank you, Cade," she says, my name sounding like warm butter melting off her lips.*

"The snow is coming down fast," she says, bringing me back to the present.

"There's no way we can make it to your cabin," I say. "I assume that's where you're going?"

"Yeah, I was."

"Are you supposed to meet anyone there?" I inquire. *Please say no.*

"No. I have some scripts to read, and Pike kind of wanted some time to himself."

"My place is closer," I say, thanking whatever divine intervention allowed her to go off the road. "You can stay there until the roads get better."

"Okay," she says with a shy smile. "Thanks for rescuing me, Cade."

"You're welcome, Palmer."

She gets in the car and shakes the snow out of her

hair. "I'm sorry about the other night. Why didn't you call me back?"

"I don't know. I just—"

"You were pissed I didn't show up, right?"

"A little."

"I sort of explained what happened in the text. Did you read it?"

"I did. Look, you know your brother hates me. He's staying at your house. It would be awkward, so I decided not to put you in that position."

"I see," she says, putting her head down.

Which makes me feel bad.

We drive in silence for a few miles then she says, "Can you even believe how gorgeous this snow is? Don't you just want to lay in it and make a bunch of snow angels?"

I grip my wheel tighter as the car fishtails on a patch of ice. "Let's hope we make it there first."

"Where are we going?" she asks. "I didn't know you had a place up here."

"I've been looking for the right place for a quite a while. Just closed a few weeks ago."

"Is it furnished? Are we going to have any food?"

"I have some basic furnishings and linens. Not much yet. I wanted to get a feel for the place before I order any more. And groceries were delivered earlier today." I turn and give her a wink. "Along with a few cases of wine."

"So we can get drunk, and we won't starve. Sounds like the perfect weekend."

I drum my fingers on the steering wheel, excited about how she mentioned the weekend. Does she want to spend the weekend with me?

Could I get so lucky?

I look over at her. Her cheeks and nose are red from the cold, but her eyes are bright with excitement about the falling snow. She's bouncing in the seat a little, like she's excited about something.

Probably just glad not to be standing on the side of the road anymore.

AFTER WINDING UP the mountain into the ski resort area of Truckee, I pull into the driveway of my new home.

"Cade! It's so pretty!" Palmer screeches. "You literally bought the house of my dreams. Don't you remember that time when I told you about it? That night when we laid under the stars in that hammock in Belize?"

I remember, alright. I remember everything about that trip. How soft her skin felt, the way her ass looked in a skimpy little bikini, the way she fit perfectly into my arms, and how amazing it felt when I was inside of her.

"We were happy then," I say flatly, the memory both blissful and painful as I open the door and pull into the garage, knowing that's why this house took years to find. When she passionately described it to me, it became my dream, too.

She jumps out of the car quickly, her face flush with excitement.

"Leave the bags, Cade. Give me a tour."

*Give me a tour.* If I had my way, a tour would involve christening each room by making love in it.

Love. Not sex. That's how it always was with Palmer. Even when the sex was completely dirty in nature, it always felt different.

I shake my head, take her outstretched hand, and follow her into the house.


AFTER GIVING HER the tour of the place, I unload our luggage, putting hers in one of the guest bedrooms and praying she'll lock herself in and read her scripts, so I won't have to keep looking at her.

Because if I have to keep looking at her, I'm going to end up fucking her.

My mother says love is based on strong emotions and that strong emotions polarize us. That's why I can both love Palmer and hate her at the same time.

And right now, I hate that I still love her.

She's standing next to one of the big picture windows, looking outside.

"The snow is really coming down now," she says. "This is crazy beautiful."

"You're crazy beautiful," I mutter.

"What?"

"I said *you're* crazy beautiful, Palmer." I say it flatly, with no emotion. I'm afraid to say it any other way.

She blushes and self-consciously pushes back a strand of hair. I love that about her. How she isn't even aware of how truly stunning she is.

"I think we need some of that wine," she says.

"Wine won't help things between us."

"No, it will probably make me want to sleep with you," she says with a sigh. Like she thinks it's a really bad idea. She walks over to the cabinet under the television and starts rummaging through it. "Do you have any cards?" She laughs, pulling out a big box. "I should have known you'd have Scrabble."

"It *is* a Crawford family tradition."

"Not *our* kind of Scrabble."

"You're right. I don't play dirty Scrabble with Mom and Dad. I've never played it with anyone but you, actually."

"So," she says, giving me a sexy grin, "shall we?"

I look out at the snow still falling heavily. "Sure, why not. You're not going anywhere for a while. I thought you had a script to read or something?"

"Scrabble sounds more *titillating*."

"I'll be impressed if you can get that word on the board. Why don't you set up the game and open some wine. I'll go get some wood and get a fire going."

ALTHOUGH THE WOOD I had delivered is stacked neatly next to the house, I wish it wasn't. Staying outside in the bristling cold wind for a few hours chopping wood might be the only thing that could keep me from kissing Palmer.

Hell, who am I kidding? I'd do way more than kiss her. Visions of carrying her to my new four-poster bed cause me to immediately harden. I slam my hand against the wall. Stop thinking about that. You can't.

*Why not?* a voice inside my head wonders.

*She hates you, for one.* Only it doesn't really seem like she hates me anymore. Not like before when she wouldn't even talk to me.

I put the wood in a carrier, take it in the house, and get a roaring fire going.

"The fire is so pretty," she says from the kitchen.

"Thanks," I reply.

"I have an idea," she says, sashaying her way toward me with a big smile on her face. Palmer's smile makes my knees weak. And I know that makes me sound like a fucking girl, but whatever, it's true.

"What's that?"

"Pick the coffee table up for me," she instructs. I pick it up while she pulls the grey shag rug out from under it and moves it right up to the fireplace. "Perfect!" she exclaims, then strips all the pillows off the couch, tossing them to the ground. She carefully places the Scrabble game on the center of the rug, bending over and giving me a great view of her incredible ass. Seriously, it's the perfect shape. If I could just strip her naked, get behind her, and grab those hips, we'd have a lot more fun than playing a stupid board game.

"I thought you might be hungry," she says, scooting the big wooden coffee table toward the rug then grabbing a tray from the kitchen and setting it down. "Cheese, crackers, smoked salmon, caviar, and caramel popcorn."

"That's quite the combination," I tease.

"I had to work with what you had. At least there's plenty of wine. Will you grab it?" she asks as she sits her ass on my rug and doles out little square letters.

I set the bottle and the glasses on the coffee table, pour the wine, and sit down across from her.

The lights flicker, then go out, enveloping the house in darkness.

She nervously twists her hair. It's an old habit, something she's done since she was a kid. I remember so clearly her lying in bed after the first time we made love, twisting her hair and wondering out loud if our sleeping together was the right thing to do.

I didn't want her to second guess us then, and I don't want her to now.

I reach out and take her hand, just like I did then. "We'll figure something out," I say, repeating the words I told her that night. Her eyes flicker with surprise at my touch, but then she softens.

"You've always known how to make me feel better," she says, gazing into my eyes and expressing more feelings than the words that came out of her mouth.

When she finally breaks eye contact, she smiles. "I don't think the lights are coming back on. I saw candles in the pantry."

"I'll grab them," I say, quickly getting up. I have to fucking do something besides stare into her eyes, or I'm going to—no. Get that out of your mind. It's not going to happen. It can't happen. Her brother hates you. You can't do that to her.

Using my phone to light the way, I get candles and matches along with a couple flashlights.

"Here, let me help you," she says, getting up and attempting to grab a couple candles from my full arms. But when her hands brush my chest, I stop and stiffen—everywhere.

"Um, that's okay, I've got them," I say, attempting to unload the candles onto the table only to have half of them topple to the ground. "Shit."

"It's okay, Cade," she says, dropping to her knees in front of me—her head now at dick-sucking level.

Fuck my life.

Why did I stop to pick her up again?

I drop down next to her, my knees sinking into the

soft rug, and set the pillars on the table. She takes the matchbox from my hand, opens it, and strikes one across the outside. Then she puts the match against the wick to light the candle. She does the same to each, and pretty soon her face is gorgeously illuminated by candlelight.

She smiles and sits back in front of the board game, pulling her legs into a pretzel.

"All good now," she says. "You ready to get this game started?"

"Uh, sure," I say, sitting down, trying to ignore how the fire is reflecting in her hair. I pick up my wine glass, needing to take a gulp.

"Shouldn't we toast first?" she asks, holding her glass up and making me feel like a manner-less idiot.

"Yes, we should. Would you like to do the honors?" Hopefully, she does. At this point, I may toast to stripping her naked and fucking her in front of the fire.

"To the knight in shining armor who saved me from freezing to death in a snowstorm, to a warm fire, a soft rug, and playing dirty Scrabble by candlelight." She touches her glass to mine then adds, "And to your beautiful new home. I hope I behave well enough to get invited back someday."

It takes everything I have not to blurt out *exactly* what kind of behavior would be sure to get her invited back. I shift uncomfortably. I've got to stop thinking about her naked.

"Cheers," I say.

"So, I guess I'll start," she says, picking up letters and placing them in the center of the board. "This one doesn't count for points, because I stole it out of the pile but I thought I'd give us a good, if not slightly ironic, start."

"Sideboob? Really?" I laugh. "You chose the word that ended us to start the game?"

She takes a large drink of wine and smirks at me. "Figured we might as well get it out in the open. We've never really talked much since then."

"I know," I say sadly, downing more wine. "Your brother—I really don't want to talk about it. I don't want to fight with you, Palmer. Not tonight. It's nice having you here with me."

"I don't want to fight with you either. I'm really sorry, Cade. I was young and stubborn back then."

"What kills me is that you never did the movie. You've never shown your boobs in *any* movie."

"I couldn't. That's what kills me, too. It was all for nothing."

"Part of what I loved about you was your stubbornness, Palmer. Your ability to go toe-to-toe with me. Or even better, Pike. Remember that summer here when you wanted to drink beer with your friends, and he had a fit?"

"Which was bullshit because he totally drank before

he was twenty-one!"

I laugh. "You got your way."

"Not always," she says, lowering her head but looking up at me through dark lashes.

*After hours chilling in the hot tub with Pike, drinking beer, and deciding which girls to invite up to the party this weekend, I'm somewhere between tipsy and drunk when I finally crawl into bed.*

*A few hours later, I'm having the best dream. Palmer's warm naked body is plastered against mine. Her lips are kissing my neck. I pull her tighter, kissing her and letting my hands caress the places I was admiring today. Her lips are as soft as I imagined. Her skin even softer. She smells of cocoa butter and rain. My tongue glides into her mouth, and our kissing is frantic, getting me all worked up. This is the best dream ever. I can't wait to—*

*"I want you to be my first, Cade," she says.*

*Wait. Hold up. What? She wouldn't say that in my dream.*

*I open my eyes with a start. Panic settles in when I find her actually in my bed, naked.*

*"What the hell are you doing in here, Palmer?" I hop out of bed. "You have to get out of here."*

*"But you're ready. I'm ready."*

*"I thought I was dreaming."*

*She smiles, happily. "You dream about me? Even better."*

*"No, fuck. No. I don't. We can't."*

*"Do you want me, Cade?" she says, pointing to my rock-hard cock. "Because it sure looks like you do."*

*"Jesus, don't say that. I don't want you. You're way too young. You're my best friend's little sister."*

*"I won't tell if you won't," she sasses, causing my dick to look like it's dancing—going from hard as a rock, to a horrified limp, and now back to ready-for-action. But then again, my dick isn't used to having a conscience. It's always ready for whatever comes my way. And when you're the star catcher and cleanup batter on your college baseball team and destined for glory, it comes in droves.*

*Even though my dick is betraying me, I repeat, "You have to get out of my room."*

*Tears fill her eyes. "Am I not pretty enough?"*

*"You're fucking gorgeous, but you're fifteen, Palmer. It's illegal. Immoral. You're my best friend's little sister. If he found out—"*

*"I swear, I would never tell."*

*"But I'd know. Please, for the love of all that is holy, you have to go."*

*She gets out of my bed, picks my baseball jersey up off the floor, madly tosses it over her head, and marches out the door with my last name, Crawford, emblazoned across her back. It's the sexiest thing I've ever seen.*

"I respect you for that," she says softly. "Hated you at the time, but now I'm glad we didn't. You would have been a bad boyfriend then."

"Who? Me?"

"Yeah, you and my brother always had a different girl. You needed to grow up before you were ready for me."

"You needed to grow up. Then on your birthday— anyway, I'll go first. I've got a good one. *Ball.*"

She takes a gulp of wine, adds eight points to my score card, and laughs. "I raise your *ball* with one *penis*. Which is eight points for me, too. We're tied."

"Speaking of tied," I tease as I refill our wine glasses, wondering where it went so fast.

"Cade!" she screeches. "Don't be naughty!"

"I'm always naughty," I say, my voice deep and throaty, my dick getting hard just remembering the time I brought home black scarves, tied her to the bedposts, and had my way with her. I remember what always made her scream. God, I want to make her scream again.

"You're just stalling because you don't have a word."

"That's where you're wrong," I say, placing tiles on the board, using the *E* from *sideboob*. "Read 'em and weep."

"*Hickey*, damn. That's like twenty-three points. I don't have shit. Oh wait!" she says, putting the word *tit* on the board.

"That's pretty small."

"Shut up. It's a double word score, so I get eight

points."

We keep playing, me adding the words *yell* and *nip* and her using the word *in* and then adding a *ples* to make *nipples out of nip*...which gives me an idea.

"Watch this," I say, setting my tiles down with flourish and adding a *ties* to the end of *tit*. *"Titties.* That's seven points and oh, look at this, two double word scores. That makes twenty-one, and I am clearly in the lead."

"Don't be so cocky," she says. "I'm just getting started. How about this? *S E X.* A double word score, adding twenty points." She pencils in her score and frowns. "You're still winning, sixty-five to forty-nine."

"Ha! Told you!" I lay down an *ratd* to the *X* in sex.

*"Xratd?* Um, no! No way!"

"But I ran out of room on the board. I think it should count."

"No." She glances down at her tiles. "Wait. I shall allow it. I mean, it's only fourteen points, right?"

"That's correct."

She gets all giddy looking, and I can tell she's got something good. She never had a poker face worth a shit. She lays down an *oggie* under my D.

"That doesn't count."

"Why not?"

"We're playing dirty Scrabble, not animal Scrabble."

*"Doggie*-style, Cade. I know you know *that* word. I'm

pretty sure that was your favorite position. Remember how you used to spank my ass?"

I gulp. Fuck. I do.

She jumps up. "And that ties us at seventy-nine! I'm going to whip you, Cade." My dick immediately jumps to full attention.

"Oh, really?" I say with a smirk. "Did you bring one?"

Her mouth hangs open. When she shuts it, she looks at me with hurt in her eyes. "We never did that. Have you? Like, with someone else?"

I quickly shake my head. I hate when she looks that way. Especially when her eyes start to get watery and fill with tears. "No, never." I reach out and touch her arm. "I was just teasing."

She swirls her wine in her glass. It's nearly empty again. She notices and refills it, polishing off the bottle.

"Looks like we need more wine," I say, getting up.

"I might need something stronger," I hear her say under her breath as I'm walking to the kitchen. I open a bottle and bring it to the table, put a couple more logs on the fire, and sit back down across the board from her.

"*Top*," I say, making my next play. "Seven points."

"*Score*," she says, putting down the tiles. "That's eight."

I lay down my next word.

"*Orgasm*," she reads, licking her lips. She closes her

eyes and takes a deep breath. "That's sixteen. Very good."

"They usually were," I tease, adding to her discomfort. I love watching her squirm. I look around at the candles flickering, the fire, the flush of her cheeks.

She ignores me and lays down two *F*s. "*Eff!* Look at that! Nine points and triple word score for twenty-seven! I'm winning!"

"You're kicking my ass. Did you see that the snow has slowed down? Hopefully that means the power will come back on soon."

She stretches her arms into the air and yawns.

"Wine always makes you sleepy." And adorable. I want to curl her into my arms and do nothing but watch her sleep. Well, after I fuck her. "Are you ready for bed?"

"Yes," she says. "Should we sleep in front of the fireplace?"

"Um, you can," I say. "I'll go in my room. I have quilts, so I will stay warm." No freaking way I can sleep next to her. She's tipsy, and I have no control where she's concerned.

"I guess if I get cold, I'll come out here," she says.

"Sounds good," I tell her. "You get to bed. I'll clean up."

She shuffles down the hallway while I put away the food and rinse the wine glasses in the sink.

Then I go to my room.

Lie in bed.

Stare at the ceiling.

And wonder just how much control I really have.

## *Palmer*

I'M TOSSING AND turning.

Turning and tossing.

There's no way I can go to sleep knowing that Cade is so close.

But he might as well be a million miles away.

I offered to sleep with him in front of the fireplace. Why did he choose his cold bed instead?

I close my eyes and will myself to sleep.

Toss and turn some more.

"This is ridiculous," I say, tossing back the covers. "We're both adults."

## *Cade*

"FUCK IT," I say, jumping out of bed.

We meet in the hall.

Stand staring at each other.

Our eyes fixed. Our bodies close.

Naked.

Neither willing to speak.

The silence screams, saying words we don't dare. It relays feelings we pretend we don't still have.

My heart is pounding so loudly, I'm sure she can hear it.

"Put your hands on me, Cade," she whispers.

I reach out, my hands starting at her shoulders, sliding down her arms, and then taking both her hands in mine. I give them a little squeeze then place them on my ass with a pat, hoping she will leave them there. I roughly caress her sides up to her neck then lower my lips to hers.

I thought if we got together again I would spend days soaking in her beauty. Hours giving her pleasure, before I would allow it for myself.

But I don't care about that right now.

I pick her up and wrap her legs around my waist, kissing her with a fervor never before felt. Leaning her against the wall, I work my fingers inside of her, our lips never parting, our tongues in a frantic battle.

"Fuck me, Cade. Please," she begs, grabbing my dick and moving it into place. I slide it in, her wetness enveloping me.

The second I do, I'm lost to her, the years fading

away.

The passion I feel now is bolder. It's audacious, dauntless. Every touch—every kiss—is familiar, but it's laced with the kind of desperation only true love can bring.

I slam into her as she breathes out my name.

"Oh, Cade. Fuck, baby. Do it harder. You know I can take it."

I curse, grab her ass, and plunge into her over and over until she's on the edge of release, then allow myself to climax.

# *Palmer*

I LEAN AGAINST the wall, breathing heavily and feeling sated, but still aflame with desire.

I weave my fingers into his hair and kiss his shoulder.

"We were always incredible together," he says, carrying me to his four-poster bed.

I stretch out, rubbing my arms against his sheets. "God, how I've missed these sheets," I say. "You even had these in college."

"How would you know that?"

"One time when I visited my brother, you weren't there. I slept in your bed. You had them when we were together, too. They are my favorite sheets ever."

"Do you have them on your bed?"

"I did, but I threw them all away when we broke up—bought the scratchy ones."

"Why?"

"Because every time I got into bed it reminded me of you, Cade. I think there's a reason why I went off the road. I think we were meant to cross paths. To end up here. You marked my soul as yours a long time ago and never let go."

"Making love to you has always been more than sex. It's like the very first time you wrapped my heart in a bungee cord and tethered it to your soul, binding me with a tenacity that no amount of time could break. No one makes me feel like you do. I love you, Palmer," he says, sliding into bed with me. "Still. I never stopped."

I grab his face and kiss him, my desire amplified by his words. His fingertips dance across my skin, igniting a fire from the lust still smoldering inside of me.

# November 2nd
## Pike

I GET A call from Carter.

"So I packed up Bethany's belongings, rented her a storage unit, and moved everything there. She's staying in my hotel room, which means I am staying at your place. Hope that's okay. Rooms are in short supply, and my client's house is full of friends and relatives in for the game."

"You're very efficient," I say, impressed.

"It's not the first time I've had to deal with a jersey chaser, Pike. I know how to take care of my clients. It's what I do."

"Sounds like I need to be one of your clients. How did she take things?"

"She was outraged. They always are until you remind them that it's because they sucked someone else's dick. I also talked to Craig about it. The guys on the team look up to you. They think what he did was shitty, but the last thing the team needs when you're playing in the Series is discord. He was shit-faced. She followed him to his room, said the two of you broke up."

"That makes me feel better, at least."

"I thought it would. Now, the real question. If they make it back to L.A. for Game Six, are you going to be there? You've got to be getting tired of moping around the house."

"That's for fucking sure."

"I know both the team owner and coach have called you, but you haven't called back."

"I haven't called anyone back."

"Why?" he asks.

"I feel like a fucking failure."

"You're not a failure, Pike. You're injured. And you're still part of this team. Start acting like it. Support them. Encourage them. They are down one game to three. If L.A. wins tonight, it's over. So, I was thinking that I'd like to take you into the clubhouse tonight."

"How?"

As he explains, I smile. For the first time since I got injured, I'm truly excited about something.

LIGHT SHINES THROUGH the curtains, waking me. Snow is fluttering down from the sky like bits of confetti. And last night wasn't a dream. Our legs are tangled, his arm is over my shoulder, his lips pressed against my temple.

It's a glorious way to start the day.

I glide my fingertips across his forearm, causing him to murmur.

"Mhm," he says, slowly opening his eyes. "What do you say we hot tub this morning? Then you can jump out and make those snow angels you love."

"Naked?" I ask, raising an eyebrow at him.

"Of course," he replies with a sexy smirk, pulling my hand to his lips and kissing it.

"Do you have any champagne?"

"For breakfast?"

"Why not?" I ask.

"Why not, indeed. You get the champagne. I'll start a fire and take the lid off the hot tub." He gives me a steamy kiss then says, "Don't take too long," and slaps my naked ass as I'm hopping out of bed.

I grab a bottle of champagne out of the wine cooler, find some orange juice, and grab a handful of bagels and a couple flutes.

The view from the deck is even more magnificent, with Cade taking center stage. There's a hint of stubble on his face, his hair is a mess, but his blue eyes are brighter than the morning sky. And the smile he gives me, if my hands weren't full, I'd put them both over my heart and try to stuff this moment into my soul.

He stands up to help empty my hands, but when he does, I practically gasp as his chest rises out of the water, and his abs come into view along with the V-line that leads down to one of the sources of my pleasure last night.

"Hurry," he says. "Aren't you cold?"

I had almost forgotten I was naked and standing outside in the snow. My body is heated simply by his smile—okay, and maybe a few other significant parts, too.

I hand him the bagels and glasses then climb into the tub, setting the bottles on the edge.

"It's a beautiful morning," I say as he pours us each a drink.

"It got even more beautiful the second you walked out on the deck. You look stunning."

I swat his arm playfully. "I know what I look like in the morning, Cade. Don't bullshit me."

"Your mascara is a tad smudged, but it just makes you look sexier. And your hair, it's total sex hair." He points to his own chest. "I made it that way."

"And that makes you proud?"

He pulls me onto his lap. "That makes me happy." He hands me my glass. "We should toast."

"To what?"

"Oh, wow. The list is long. Be prepared. This is going to take awhile." Because I'm sitting on him, there isn't much room between us for the flutes, so they are pressed against our chests. "To surprise blizzards. To your car sliding off the road. To my rescuing you. To dirty Scrabble. To wine. To not being able to sleep knowing you were so close to me. To you being in the hall. As a matter of fact, to the hall itself. To my new four-poster bed. To my soft sheets. To the way your skin feels pressed against mine. To the way you sound when you come. To multiple orgasms. To the way your lips feel when they're wrapped around my dick. How it feels to slide inside you. To rough, dirty fucking. To passionate, sweet love making. To waking up with you. To you naked. And really, mostly to how fucking happy you make me. Cheers."

I am blushing through most of it, but after taking of sip of champagne, I boldly tilt my hips upward, so we can be joined again.

"I need your cock inside me, now," I say with a laugh.

"Why are you laughing? That is not a laughing matter."

"Because when you asked me if there was anything I needed after being at the hospital, Tory told me that's how I should have answered."

"Fuck yeah," he says, kissing me again and slowly moving inside me. "That will *always* be the right answer."

I chug my drink and set it on the edge of the hot tub then run my hands through his beautiful hair. Sex last night took place mostly in the dark. Now, we are out in full daylight, our gazes locked, our feelings and bodies on full display. Thankfully, the hot tub is fairly secluded, but even if it weren't, I wouldn't care. He's my sole focus.

What starts out slow, quickly heats up, our bodies moving at a more frantic pace, both reaching for ecstasy.

"Damn, girl," Cade whispers against my neck when he climaxes and drops his head to my shoulder, kissing it.

"Getting too old to keep up with me?" I tease. "I mean, you're in your thirties now. You're getting to be an old man."

"I've always been an old man compared to you, Rookie," he teases.

"Are you too old for naked snow angels?"

"The ski trail goes right by the house. With all the powder, I'm sure it will be busy."

"Then a lot of skiers will see my naked ass making a snow angel." I stand up, hop out of the tub, and grab his hand. "Come with me, Cade."

He takes my hand and says, "Always."

I scream as we run through the snow on the deck, down the stairs, and to the backyard. He grabs me around the waist and tackles me into the snow. "Ahh! That's so cold!"

"I think it feels good. You keep getting me hot."

I pull away from him, quickly make a snow angel, and then run screaming back upstairs, the snow feeling so cold on my feet it almost burns. I start to ease into the hot tub, but Cade picks me up and carries me into the house, lying on top of me in front of the fire and then covering us with a blanket.

"It's my understanding that body heat is the most effective way to get warm."

"I'll bet it is," I agree, putting my lips against his chest.

AFTER MAKING LOVE by the fire, we decide to go skiing. We can't let the perfect powder go to waste.

## Pike

I PREP FOR tonight like I'm actually playing in the game. Shower—well, a sink shower, shave, and put on a suit. Well, actually, I can't put on the suit pants, and I don't want to cut up the leg, so I put on shorts.

Then I decide I feel ridiculous.

I find the plastic bag from the hospital with my clothes in it and put on the shirt.

Then I get myself set up in front of the computer for

the teleconference that will be beamed into the club-house.

When I see my teammates' faces in the locker room, I start speaking.

"I'll admit, many of you have called me, sent texts and well wishes, and I haven't replied to any of them. Because I felt like I let you all down. I felt like I failed. I was reminded today that I'm still part of this team, and that I need to start acting like it. I got hurt. Big fucking deal. We all get hurt at some point in our career. We suck it up, rehab, and keep going back out there. I was going to address you all in a suit, like I would before a normal game, but it didn't feel right. You'll notice I'm wearing the jersey I wore when I got hurt. It's dirty. Full of blood, sweat, and tears. And they are all mine. Look down at your jersey right now. Tonight those jerseys don't just represent your city. Your team. Your jersey represents the culmination of your career. The hours you've spent practicing and playing since you were a kid. The blood, sweat, and tears *you've* left on every ball field you've ever played on." I pause briefly, collecting myself.

"We're down three games to one, and I have just one more thing to say to you. Don't you fucking dare let them win the series in *our house*. You're coming back to L.A. for games six and seven, and I'm going to be in the dugout with you. And we're going to make everything these jerseys represent worth it."

My teammates look emotional then cheer and head out to the field.

And I feel like myself again.

OUR TEAM WINS Game Five, and I am so incredibly pumped about it. The series is now two to three, meaning Tampa is coming back to L.A.

# Cade

WE GET BACK from skiing, take a sexy shower, have fun making pasta together, and end up back in the hot tub. Honestly, my body needs it. It's gotten an extreme workout in the last twenty-four hours.

Not that I'm complaining.

I put my arm out, and Palmer snuggles into it, fitting perfectly as usual. That's one thing about us that always amazed me—how perfectly we fit together. I've been with a lot of women over the years, but no one has fit the way she does. Like we're two pieces split apart at birth who found their way back to each other. I wonder if that's what soul mates are. Some predestined pairing.

Now that the snowstorm is gone, the night is cloudless and there are a billion stars in the sky. While Palmer is stargazing, I'm Palmer-gazing. Just staring at her beautiful profile, the way her wet hair is curling around her face, the splay of lashes on her cheeks when she blinks, the rosiness of her high cheekbones.

"Ohmigosh, Cade! Look! A shooting star!"

"I see it!"

"I've never seen one before," she says.

"It's a sign," I tell her, caressing her arm.

"What do you mean?"

"We just had another first together. I want the rest of my firsts with you, Palmer."

She turns away from me.

"What's wrong?"

When she turns back to face me, there are tears in her eyes.

"Why are you crying?"

"I'm just so happy. I can't believe I'm sitting here with you. I was afraid it wouldn't be as good. Or that it would be good, and we'd only do it once, and it'd be over. That you'd think I got fat. I don't know. It's like all at once every single insecurity I have has come out. I don't want this to be just a stuck-in-the-snow thing."

"We've wasted too much time apart," I tell her.

"We have amazing chemistry."

"Is that another way of saying the sex is mind-blowing?"

Well, someone was blowing something," she says, naughtily. I love her playfulness.

"There was a lot of mutual satisfaction, I think," I tease back. But then I take her face in my hands, wipe her tears away, and speak from my heart. "Palmer, I've been in love with you for most of my life. As far as I'm concerned, this isn't just a stuck-in-the-snow thing. This is a together forever thing."

She smiles at me, but more tears fall. She throws her arms around my neck. "I love you, Cade."

"I love you, too."

# November 3rd
## *Palmer*

"I DIDN'T HEAR you come in last night," Pike says, rolling into the kitchen.

"I took the red-eye. Slept in. Look at all these flowers! I take it people now know where you're staying. How are you feeling? I heard Tampa won last night. Do you still want to go to the game tomorrow?"

"Absolutely. How was Tahoe? Did you get your scripts read?"

"What scripts?"

"The scripts you went up there to read?"

"Oh, yeah. They were really *amazing*."

"So you're planning on doing a deal?"

"Definitely," I say dreamily, not at all talking about the scripts.

"Which ones did you like? And what did you like about them?" Tory inquires, joining us in the kitchen. "Are you interested in any of them for yourself?"

"Oh, yes, very."

"You're acting really strange," Pike states.

"No, I'm not. I'm just in a good mood."

"Good enough to take me out to dinner tonight?" he asks. "I'm dying for a big steak."

"It's a date," I tell him.

THE DOORBELL RINGS, and Tory goes to answer it, explaining, "We have another delivery. I just let them in the gate."

She runs to the door and comes back into the kitchen with a large box, setting it on the island. "It's for you, Palmer. What is it?"

"I don't know," I say, undoing the ribbon and taking off the lid.

My eyes get huge when I see what's inside. "Oh my gosh! They're better than roses!"

"What's that?" my brother asks, rolling himself over to take a closer look.

"Sheets!" I say excitedly, opening the package and rubbing the soft fabric across my cheek, remembering.

"You're grinning. Who are they from?" Tory wants to know.

I don't have to look at the card to know the answer. "Cade," I say proudly, wondering how Pike will react to hearing his name.

"Why is that asshole sending you sheets?"

"There was a blizzard when I was driving to the house. The streets were slick. I slid off the road. Cade happened to be driving by and rescued me."

"Why didn't you call a tow truck?"

"I did, but they couldn't get there for at least an hour."

"So he drove you to the house?"

"No, it was too far. And the roads were a mess. He took me to his house."

"And?"

"And I stayed there."

"And?" he says, his face turning red.

"And, all of his rooms have these sheets. They were so soft I said I that I wanted to get some, so I guess he decided to send them."

"He's still a fucking prick," he says in an irritated tone as he rolls away.

## Cade

I GET AN email from the service letting me know the gift was delivered to Palmer's house. I thought about sending her flowers, but this seemed more appropriate.

She calls me.

"I got your gift. I just have one problem with it."

"What's that?"

"I'm hoping they don't mean that I won't be invited

to sleep on your sheets now that I have a set of my own."

"I was a little worried Pike might get mad at you. Did you tell him anything?"

"I told him we hooked up, and it was amazing."

"Palmer! What the hell?"

"I'm joking. I didn't tell him anything other than you rescued me, and your new house has great sheets. It's none of his business what I do."

"I should talk to him."

"You should, but not now. I'm too happy."

"I'm happy, too. I love you."

"I love you, too."

"Can I see you tonight?"

"I promised Pike I'd take him out to dinner."

"After?"

"Hmm, maybe I'll put him to bed and sneak over to yours?"

"I'll be waiting all day for that."

"I had another first with you last night, Cade."

"What's that?"

"The Mile High Club," she purrs. "That was fun."

"I wholeheartedly agree. The weekend was fun. All of it."

# November 5th
## *Palmer*

"THAT GAME LAST night, can you believe Tampa pulled it off?" Tory asks, wandering into the kitchen this morning.

"It was amazing!" I add, although, honestly, I didn't watch it. Pike went to the game, so Cade came over to properly break in my new sheets. Even though he left before Pike got home, I lingered in bed for longer than usual this morning because my sheets smell like Cade.

I can't even believe how happy I am.

But I'm sad about one thing. That I can't share my happiness with my brother. At some point, I need to grow a set of balls and just tell him. Just maybe not while he's staying at my house.

"The phone and doorbell have been ringing off the hook with interview requests and gifts for Pike," Tory says. "I feel like I haven't been getting a whole lot of work done the past few days."

"That's okay," I say dreamily, knowing I have lunch plans that involve getting naughty on Cade's desk. It's something I've always wanted to do, but never have. And if we're going to have more firsts . . . "You go ahead and help him. I don't have anything pressing."

"No, but you've got a full schedule today," she says, handing me a sheet of paper. "Hair and makeup at nine, radio interview at eleven, meeting at the studio to pitch your latest production project at two-thirty—"

"Then I'm going to the game with my brother," I finish for her.

"Actually, I have interviews pre-game," Pike yells in from the family room couch. "I have to be there early. Can you meet me there? Tory has your VIP tickets and all the details."

"I can do that," I say, making myself a quick smoothie and heading out the door.

# Cade

"I CAN BE at your office at twelve-thirty," Palmer says when she calls me. "Will you be free?"

"Like for lunch? Sure. Do you just want me to meet you somewhere?"

"No, I'll meet you there, and I'll bring lunch. Don't ask questions."

"Uh, okay. See you then, I guess. Is everything okay,

Palmer?"

"Everything is perfect, Cade."

A FEW HOURS later, she shows up looking like a total smoke show, even though she's wearing a very demure shirtwaist dress with high heels like a sixties housewife.

She shuts the door behind my assistant, leans against it, and not-so discreetly locks it, giving me a tempestuous smile as she approaches my desk.

"What are you up to, Miss Montlake?"

"What makes you think I'm up to something, Mr. Crawford?" she purrs.

"Because you walked in here looking like a sex kitten, locked the door, and you don't seem to have brought any lunch."

She takes out the clip holding up her hair, shaking it as it falls over her shoulders.

I start to rise, in more ways than one.

"Don't get up. It's not time for lunch yet." She unbuttons her dress, slowly revealing slivers of skin and red lace.

When she lets the dress slide down to the floor and steps toward me, I stand and hold my hand out toward her.

Her long legs are encased in nude colored stockings held in place by a red garter with a matching thong. Her slim waist is highlighted by a red lace bustier, the cups see-through, allowing me a peek of her sensational breasts.

I feel myself harden as she leans across the desk. I mimic her move and am rewarded with a steamy kiss.

I push against the edge of the desk, willing it to disappear.

Palmer turns away from me, plops her fine ass on my desk, then spins around toward me, so that her legs are now spread eagle in front of me.

Eager with anticipation, I undo my belt and grasp my zipper. She stands, her high heels bringing us almost face to face, while she unzips my pants for me.

When they hit the floor, she drops to her knees in front of me, pushes off my boxer briefs, and wraps her hand around the base of my cock while tracing the tip with her tongue. My dick grows harder when she takes it fully into her mouth. She guides me in and out, pleasuring me until I'm ready to burst.

I pull back, causing her to look up at me through her long eyelashes.

"I want you to fuck me on your desk today, because it's something we've never done before. But just now I realized that we never even kissed in your office once, let alone sucked and fucked."

"If you keep doing that, I'm going to—"

"I know exactly what you'll do, Cade," she replies, getting up off her knees, slipping out of her panties and tossing them aside.

Then she hops her naked ass back onto my desk and spreads her legs, allowing me entry.

I don't need an engraved invitation.

I grab her thighs, pushing them further apart and drop to my knees, pulling her wetness to my lips. I circle her clit with my tongue then bury it inside of her. After giving her a good tongue fucking, I slide two fingers inside her while I suck her clit, quickly sending her over the edge.

She leans back and lets out a throaty moan.

I can't take it any longer. I'm going to blow my load just watching her orgasm. Her back is arched, her head tipped back, her mouth open and crying out my name. It's sexy as fuck.

I remove my fingers from her and replace them with my dick, slamming into her glistening wetness with ease. She tightens, giving my dick a gentle squeeze that nearly undoes me.

"Oh fuck, Cade. That feels so good. Your fingers are incredible, but nothing can top having your hard dick inside of me." She grabs the back of my neck and pulls me toward her, forcing me to stay motionless inside her. She kisses me, our tongues playing an exquisite game of tug-of-war. I move my lips to her neck, knowing she loves the way it tickles. She lets out a sweet giggle then wraps her long legs around me, allowing me deeper access into her warmth.

"You have a dirty mouth," I say, tugging at her lip.

"And you love it."

God, do I. This woman turns me on.

Usually I'd start slowly and pick up the pace, but I'm beyond that point. I grab her ass, plunging in and out of her until we're both gasping for air and begging each other for release.

My breath speeds up then I groan deeply, a guttural sound I can't control as I climax, falling limply on top of her.

She catches her breath then trails her lips slowly across my neck.

"That was the best lunch I've ever had," she whispers in my ear. "You know all those times we met in your office, this is all I could think about."

I pull her up to a sitting position and glide my knuckles across her bustier. "This lacy stuff is really pretty."

"Pretty or hot?"

"Fucking hot, Palmer. And so you know, just because I wouldn't do anything with you in my office, doesn't mean I haven't thought about it. In fact, doing you on my desk has always been my biggest fantasy."

I pull out of her and dispose of the condom.

"I didn't even know you slid that on. Thank goodness someone was thinking clearly," she says, picking up her dress.

I swipe it out of her hands and help put it on, buttoning each one of the tiny buttons. Then I pick her thong up off the floor.

"I'm keeping this here," I say, dropping it into my desk drawer.

"Like a trophy?"

"Exactly like a trophy. Just because—"

"Tell me about it. Your fantasy," she says, her eyes bright and wide.

I pick her up, carry her to my couch, and sit down with her in my lap.

"Do you remember when you stopped by my office late one night on the way to a party?"

"I do. It was my first celebrity party as an actress. I had just started filming my first movie."

"You looked like you'd been out in the sun that day, because the freckles sprinkled across your nose were darker. Your hair was in a messy side braid. You had that fresh-faced innocent look people fell in love with. *I* fell in love with."

"Do you remember what I was wearing?"

"Oh, yeah. Talk about a walking contradiction. You had on a pale pink dress. Even the color screamed sweetness. Except that it looked liked bandages were wrapped tightly around your body, and it was cut so low. And you had on silver stilettos. Freaking took my breath away."

"You asked me to stop by to sign a contract."

"And when you asked me for a pen, you looked straight at my crotch."

She giggles and runs her hand through my hair. "Silly, that's because you were standing, and the pen was on your desk—at crotch level."

"Yeah, bullshit. You were trying again to seduce me."

"Next time I come for lunch, I'm braiding my hair and wearing that dress."

"The next time you come at lunch, is going to be in a few minutes," I tease, sliding my hand back under her dress.

## *Pike*

I'M IN THE clubhouse with the team. I've been thinking all day about what I could say that would motivate them. About what motivates me. The series is tied three to three, and tonight's game decides which team will win.

I wheel myself into the center of the room. I had a speech planned, but as I look down at my leg, I change my mind.

"I was asked to say something that would motivate you all. A rah-rah speech. But I ain't no fucking cheerleader. I've played on a whole lot of teams in my career, but this team has something special that our opponent doesn't have. We're a team. What that means is we're not about a few hotshots like they are. Every single guy on our team is a standout. Every single guy here is good at his job." I motion to the first baseman. "Will you help me unwrap the bandage from around my leg?"

"Uh, sure, Pike," he says, carefully unwinding it and exposing the cast-like splints on each side.

"I'd like each of you to sign this splint," I say, pointing to one of them.

The guys look confused, wondering what the heck is going on, but do as I ask and sign it.

"You're probably wondering why I had you do that. This is why. When we come back to this clubhouse after the game, I'm going to take these splints off and I'm going to hang them on the wall for L.A. to see. I want them to know that it didn't matter that they took one of us out. It didn't matter, because *every single player* on this team is a standout. And guess what we're going to write on the other splint."

"World Series Champions!" the team yells in unison.

"You fucking got that right. Because when we come back here, to this very spot, that's exactly what we're going to be! Now get out there and kick some ass!"

# Cade

IT'S THE BOTTOM of the ninth inning, bases loaded, one out. Tampa is leading the game four runs to two.

Los Angeles' batter takes a few practice swings then steps inside the box. The pitcher winds up and throws a fastball straight down the middle.

Strike one.

The catcher throws the ball back and flashes the signal. The pitcher throws, and the batter swings and connects—a grounder to the shortstop.

The shortstop throws it to the second baseman for the out. The second baseman then turns and quickly throws out the runner at first.

"Double play!" the announcer yells. "Tampa has won! Tampa has won! Tampa has won the World Series!"

Carter and I cheer like crazy. We watched the majority of the game from a sky box, but in anticipation of the end of the game, we moved closer to the field.

As we make our way onto it, the winning team gang tackles the men who made the double play. The players and coaches rush out to join them in celebration.

All except for Pike, who is sitting in the dugout, his head down.

"Aw, fuck," I say, knowing exactly how he feels.

*The team rushes the mound, jumping on Pike and ending up in a pile on the dirt.*

*I can't run out with the team, so I just stand on one foot, clapping and cheering.*

*As I watch them celebrate, I'm overcome with emotion. We've all worked so hard for this. I can't believe we actually won and are College World Series Champions.*

*I put my head down for a moment and say a grateful prayer.*

*When I look up, a dusty-uniformed Pike is standing in front of me.*

*"Come on, bud. You gotta be part of the celebration. We wouldn't be here if it weren't for you." He and a teammate lift me onto their shoulders and carry me out onto the field.*

"What do you say, Carter?" I ask, pointing at Pike. "Will you help me?"

Carter fist bumps me, remembering. "I'd say you owe him."

We rush over to the dugout.

"Come on, bud," I say to Pike. "You gotta be part of the celebration. They wouldn't be here if it weren't for you."

We don't really wait for an answer. We lift him onto our shoulders and carry him out to the field.

# *Pike*

CONFETTI RAINS DOWN on me. Players congratulate each other.

I'm overcome with emotion.

And it's more than the thrill of victory. As I sit atop Cade and Carter's shoulders celebrating with my team, I realize that for the first time in years, my life feels right.

# *Palmer*

I'M RUNNING WITH the players' families onto the field, looking for my brother, as the confetti rains down.

When I finally spot him, I stop dead in my tracks.

Carter and Cade have lifted him up on their shoulders and are carrying him out on the field—just like my brother did for Cade so many years ago.

I put my head down, mourning the loss of their friendship.

And knowing I caused it.

But as I continue to watch them, noticing the grins on their faces, I realize that maybe, just maybe, there is hope that they might overcome it.

# Pike

AFTER THE TROPHY is given to us, the interviews are finished, the fans are applauded, and the confetti settles down, the team makes its way to the clubhouse.

Goggles are handed to us as we go inside. The lockers are covered in plastic in preparation for this.

Magnums of champagne are being guzzled and sprayed. Teammates are cheering, hugging, and pouring full bottles of champagne on each other's heads.

Everyone is soaked.

The music is turned up.

Coach holds up the trophy and more champagne flies. Players take turn holding the trophy and getting doused with champagne.

This goes on for at least an hour. Finally, everyone settles down, the win actually sinking in.

"We did it," a player says. "I can't believe we actually did it."

"I've been dreaming of this day since I was a kid," another says.

The team trainer helps me take off the splint everyone signed. I hold it up into the air to more cheers and then it's hung on the wall. The words *World Series Champs* are drawn graffiti-style on the other splint and added to the top.

I stand up on one leg and yell out, "Somebody get

me a fucking boot!"

# Cade

PALMER AND I meet up after the team goes to the clubhouse.

"Need a lift?" I ask her. "I've got a limo."

"That sounds great," she says.

She's quiet in the car.

I put my hand on her knee. "What are you thinking about?"

"What you did for Pike," she says, tearing up, "was beautiful."

"I don't know about beautiful. He was hurt. I helped him. That's what teammates do."

"Except that you're not teammates anymore. You're not even friends. And it's all my fault. How can you not hate me for it?"

"Palmer, let's not get into this right now. It's been an amazing night. Your brother just won his first Series."

"See, you saying that tells me that you do!"

"I don't hate you."

"But you did."

"Sure, I did! I loved you, and your brother was my best friend. When you broke up with me, not only did I lose the love of my life, I lost my best friend, too. But I take equal blame. I should have told him how I felt about you years before that."

"How did you feel?" she whispers.

"Like we belonged together."

"I still feel that way, Cade."

"I do, too." I wrap my arm around her and enjoy that moment when she melts into my shoulder. She's worth fighting for. "And I don't care what anyone, including your brother, thinks. This is about our happiness, and we deserve to be happy. Starting now."

# November 6th
## *Palmer*

"DID YOU SEE this?" I ask Tory, turning on the TV in my office.

"I saw it live last night," she says, "I thought it was—"

"Folks," the announcer says, running a video clip. "This is the All-Star pitcher, Pike Montlake, whose fastball has inspired young pitchers around the world. As you all know, he suffered a horrific ankle and leg break in the first game of the Series. But he was back last night, cheering on his team. When that double play was made for the win, the team ran out onto the field. Everyone except for Pike, who is in a wheelchair. Now watch as two men come down from the stands, lift Pike onto their shoulders, and carry him out to celebrate.

"What you may not remember is that this same scene played out in similar fashion in another big game fifteen years earlier. It's the final game in the College World Series. Pike Montlake has pitched a nearly perfect game. A pop fly to centerfield means the runner on third tags up and takes off. And on this play, major league draft pick Cade Crawford is injured and carted off the field.

"With the bases loaded and a back-up catcher, Pike throws three beautiful fastballs across home plate, for the strike out and the win. Pike is tackled on the mound, but watch what he does. He grabs a teammate, runs to the dugout, and puts a booted-up Crawford on their shoulders. The man last night who carried Pike onto the field to celebrate with his team was none other than Cade Crawford. This scene right here is why baseball is America's sport. A sport that goes beyond apple pie and hotdogs. It's the brotherhood and the friendships, that are formed on the Little League fields. It's the camaraderie. The love—felt in every city and country in our great land. Congratulations, Tampa, you are the World Series Champions!"

"You're crying," Tory says, wiping tears from her own eyes.

"I ruined that friendship," I tell her.

"From what I saw, it looks like it's still there."

"Maybe."

"Did Pike say anything about it?"

"He didn't come home last night. They moved the party from the clubhouse to the hotel. Then he went straight to interviews this morning."

"Oh, look!" Tory says, "He's on now!"

"Quick, turn it back up!" I say, as she fumbles with the remote.

"It's great to have you here, Pike," the sportscaster says. "You just watched those touching scenes. Can you tell me how it feels to have your lifelong friend return a fifteen-year-old favor?"

Pike scratches his forehead, then says, "It felt really great, Chad. Really great."

"Aww," Tory says, "he's all choked up. That's so sweet. I love baseball."

"You never watch baseball."

"I didn't realize it was so emotional," she says, fanning her face. "Plus, I met this guy at the bar last night who is in the minor leagues. Talk about a hottie."

The interviewer says to Pike, "And we heard a rumor about your future."

Pike says coyly, "Which one?"

"That you're in talks with L.A. to become their pitching coach. You going to take them up on it?"

"I'm under contract with Tampa, and we just won the World Series. That's what we should be talking about. Not to mention the fact that I'm not sure how my injury will affect my career."

"Okay, let's talk hypothetically. You decide to retire. Then what?"

Pike gives him a wide smile. "Well, I am a So Cal boy. I'd love to come back home, eventually."

"Wow," I say. "Just the other day he was telling me he wanted to buy a house on the Gulf."

"Maybe he thought that was his only option," Tory says. "Speaking of options." She flashes me her phone. "Which guy should I hang out with tonight? This one or this one?"

"What the hell, Tory?" I scream. "Those are dick pictures!"

"Nothing wrong with checking out the package before you buy the product," she giggles.

# November 7th
## *Pike*

THE DAYS FOLLOWING the World Series win are a whirlwind of celebrations and interviews. The side-by-side shots of Cade and I are still playing on the news. We've become the poster children for what baseball is all about.

I was told Cade turned down numerous requests to be interviewed alongside me.

I realize that when I punched him six years ago, it didn't really settle anything. I'll never forget how mad I felt when my sister told me what he'd done. We've never talked about why he did what he did. Not that there is any possible acceptable excuse, but we've never spoken since that day.

And it still hurts.

Hurts that he would do something like that to me. That our friendship and my sister meant so little to him that it was worth throwing away on something that was probably meaningless.

It's also not something the Cade I knew would have

ever done. He was always the responsible one. The thoughtful one.

If I would have been asked to choose a man for my sister to marry, he would have been a man like Cade.

But I guess you never know.

I shake my head and look out at the nearly five-hundred-thousand people who have turned out in Tampa for the parade to celebrate our victory.

# November 12th
## *Palmer*

MY BROTHER HAS been in Florida celebrating with his team but is due back home today.

Cade and I haven't talked about my brother, but their story is splashed everywhere and is hard to get away from. Cade has gotten numerous requests for interviews about it. When I asked him why he turned them down, he said that it would be awkward. That he couldn't go on TV and talk about why he did what he did.

He saw something, owed something, and reacted.

And then he told me that he didn't want to discuss it anymore.

I could see the hurt in his eyes, so I finally dropped it.

Because I haven't been this happy in years.

Cade makes me feel whole—complete—again. The pieces of me I left with him that day I stormed out, are back where they belong.

I replay last night in my mind.

*"We're so lucky, Palmer," he says, slowly trailing his*

*finger down my side as we're cuddling post-sex.*

*"Why's that?" I ask dreamily, resting my head on his shoulder. Even though I know the answer, I want to hear him say it.*

*"Because we found our way back to each other."*

*"More like you found me in a snowstorm," I tease.*

*His finger stops on my hip. "Can I ask you a serious question?"*

*I look into his eyes and nod.*

*"If I ask you to marry me again, will you say yes?"*

*I smile at him, but don't reply. I'm so incredibly happy, but the guilt is starting to consume me.*

*How can I agree to a happily ever after with Cade when things are the way they are between him and my brother?*

*Cade brushes his fingers through my hair and smiles. "Are you free this Saturday night?"*

*"I am."*

*"Good," he says, his lips gliding across my cheek. "Because we're going to have another first date."*

"I've got all sorts of goodies for you," Tory says, bursting through the door to my office and setting a kale smoothie on my desk.

I turn my nose up to the nasty green looking concoction. "No chocolate chip Frappuccino today?"

"I wouldn't think so. You have that cover shoot for the fitness magazine as soon as you get back from New York." I glance down at my calendar to check out my busy schedule and notice the little red star marked on yesterday's square—meaning I should be getting my period anytime now—as she holds out a pure white bikini and says, "And this is what you'll be wearing."

Great.

"I called your stylist" she says. "She'll be over shortly with options for you to try for your press junket. Are you so excited for this movie to release?"

I shrug. "Honestly, I didn't realize it was this week, but I also didn't realize it's already the middle of November. It's been crazy since Pike got hurt."

"And I was thinking it's been crazy since you got the sheets." She raises an eyebrow at me. "You're sleeping with Cade, aren't you?"

I sigh.

She points her finger at me. "I knew it! And you should be proud of me. I didn't say anything in front of your brother, because it's obvious you don't want him to know."

"How obvious?"

"You hugged the sheets and said they were better than roses...that and the fact that you've been on cloud nine since then—what can I say? I'm intuitive. Speaking of that—I was right to choose the guy in dick pic two. We totally meshed."

"Meshed?" I ask as my phone buzzes on my desk. "What does that even mean?"

"It means he was fucktacular. Have you ever had sex so good it was like you were tripping? Like it was almost fuckadelic?"

"Is that even a word?"

"Probably. You get my meaning though, right?"

"Yes, I get your meaning." I smile at my phone, seeing Cade's name pop up.

"Answer the question," she says, grabbing my phone.

"Maybe?"

"Fucktacular is so spectacular there are no words to properly describe its hotness. If you had it, you'd know. Is it that way with Cade?"

My face breaks out into a grin, before I can stop myself.

Tory points at me. "Ha! I knew it! So what are you going to do about him and your brother? Should we set up a playdate so they can become best friends again? Have they talked?"

"They haven't. Everyone wanted to interview them together, but Cade turned them down."

"Why?"

"I'm not sure," I admit, "but I think he is waiting for Pike to apologize."

"Is that ever going to happen?"

I shake my head as tears form. "I don't think so."

"Why are you crying?"

"Because I'm so incredibly happy with Cade, I can

hardly stand it. But I'm not sure if I can be with someone my brother hates, no matter what Cade says."

"What did he say?"

"He said our happiness is all that matters."

"He's right," she says, handing me back my phone. "The rest will work itself out."

"Do you really think so?" I ask, clutching the phone to my chest.

"Yeah, Palmer. I do," she says as her phone rings, alerting us to the fact that my stylist is here.

While she answers the door, I read the text.

**Cade:** I miss you and desperately need to see you before you leave.

**Me:** I wish I could. The stylist is bringing clothes for me to try on. I have an hour and a half to choose them and pack before I have to leave for the airport.

**Cade:** Then I'll text you constantly until Saturday. I know how busy press junkets are. You don't even have to reply.

**Me:** It's nice that you understand.

**Cade:** Of course, I do.

**Me:** I'll miss you, but can't wait for our second "first" date when I get back.

**Cade:** I love you.

**Me:** I love you, too.

Upon arrival in New York, I'm shuttled from one event to the other. When I'm finally in my hotel room, I lie in bed and text Cade.

**Me:** *It's been a long day. How was yours?*

**Cade:** *I've spent all day thinking about you.*

**Me:** *Have they been naughty thoughts?*

**Cade:** *Actually, no. I've got it so bad for you I may start writing poetry.*

**Me:** *I doubt you have it that bad. LOL*

**Cade:** *At the touch of love, everyone becomes a po-et.—Plato*

**Me:** *You're too cute.*

# November 13th
## Cade

I SPEND ENTIRELY too much time today trying to find the perfect quote to send to Palmer. I know press junkets mean she will be interviewed all day. When she doesn't have interviews, she and the rest of the cast will be excepted to attend other events until they drop into bed for the night—only to get up and do it again the next day. I find one that seems fitting and send it off.

**Me:** *The heart that truly loves never forgets.—Proverb*

She doesn't reply until after midnight, East coast time.

**Palmer:** *That's beautiful and very much us. I love you.*

# November 14th
## *Cade*

I GLANCE AT my watch and see it's already almost seven. No wonder my stomach is growling. Time to close up shop for the day and get some dinner. Carter should be here any minute. But first, I need to call my mom and get a recipe. I'm going to cook Palmer dinner tomorrow night and something from a restaurant or out of the freezer won't cut it.

"Hey, Mom," I say, when she answers. "Can I get your recipe for spaghetti and meatballs."

"I'd be happy to make them for you, Cade," she replies.

"I know, I just—I sort of have a date tomorrow night, and I want to cook for her."

"You're turning into a girl," Carter says from my doorway.

I flip him off.

"Well, that's very nice, dear," Mom says. "Would that date happen to be Palmer?"

"Uh, why would you think that?"

"Mothers have a sixth sense about these things."

"Oh. Yeah, kinda."

"It's kinda for her, Cade? Or it *is* for her?"

"It is."

"Very well, then. I'll email you both the recipe and a shopping list."

"Thanks, Mom," I say as Carter sits in the chair in front of my desk.

When I hang up, he gives me a smirk.

"What?"

"Cooking for Palmer. Sounds serious."

"It might be." I shake my head. "I mean, I think it is. I hope it is."

"Does that mean you and Pike made up?"

"No. That's not going to happen."

"Why not? You carried him out on the field. If there was ever a time to talk, it's now."

"If he wanted to talk, he'd call me. But I don't care what Pike thinks anymore. I just want to be happy, and Palmer makes me happy."

"Then that makes me happy," he says, even though I can tell he doesn't agree.

When I get home from dinner, I go a little crazy with the love quotes.

> **Me:** She walks in beauty, like the night of cloudless climes and starry skies.—Lord Byron
>
> **Me:** Soul meets soul on lovers' lips.—Percy Bysshe

*Shelley*

**Me:** *Love is of all passions the strongest, for it attacks simultaneously the head, the heart, and the senses.—Lao Tzu, philosopher*

**Me:** *I love thee, I love but thee*
*With a love that shall not die*
*Till the sun grows cold*
*And the stars grow old.—William Shakespeare*

My phone rings, waking me.

"Sorry, it's so late," the object of my affection whispers into my ear.

"You just getting in?"

"Yes. I may fall asleep on you tomorrow night."

"I have no problem with that," I tease.

"I love the quotes, Cade. You're sweet."

"I'm pathetic is what I am. I miss you."

"I know, it's like I just got you back and then I had to leave. Bad timing. Even though I couldn't reply, I could see your texts and they kept a smile on my face all day long."

"That makes me happy. You sound exhausted. Go to sleep."

"I am. Love you."

"Love you too, Rookie."

"Isn't it about time I move up to the big leagues?" she teases.

"Yeah, it is. Goodnight."

"Goodnight, Cade."

AFTER WE HANG up, I think about what she said. She's ready to move up to the big leagues with me. Which is a good thing, since I plan on proposing tomorrow night. Crazy, I know. But I don't want to waste any more precious time without her.

# November 15th
## *Palmer*

I'M PACKING AND getting ready for my flight home. It was a crazy few days. Because the movie is a romantic comedy about a trio of girlfriends living in New York City, they held the press junket here. The studio flew in hundreds of reporters, put them up in a gorgeous hotel, screened the movie, and made the cast available for interviews. We spent the first day going from room to room, or table to table, almost like speed dating, giving each group about fifteen minutes of our time.

The next day we talked to the TV reporters who the studio decided warranted one-on-one time. The good thing about these interviews is that I get to stay put, and the journalists rotate in. We don't get to talk long, though. They are rotated through every five minutes, each bringing their own camera man and lighting. So basically I had to say the same things and answer the same questions hundreds of times while trying to remain upbeat, fun, and polite.

Needless to say, I'm ready to get home. Especially

when I get another love text from Cade.

> **Cade:** *We're like two pieces split apart at birth who found their way back to each other. We're soul mates—a predestined pairing.*

As I'm getting into the car that's driving me to the airport, I get another.

> **Cade:** *Since we broke up, I've been living a pretty rigid life, trying to make myself feel in control. It's all an illusion though. My life only feels centered when she's in it.*

Once I'm situated on the plane, I notice something. I scroll back and look at his other texts and wonder why he didn't mention who wrote them.

> **Cade:** *I am stupidly in love with this girl.*
> **Me:** *Who wrote these three?*
> **Cade:** *Me. For you.*

I reread them with tears in my eyes.

> **Me:** *I love them. And I love you. Getting ready to take off. Can't wait to see you tonight.*

When I get home, I immediately unpack, hoping it will make me feel like my life is in order.

Press junkets are always exhausting, but I'm more tired than usual. I think I may be coming down with something, which wouldn't be much of a surprise considering all the hands I shook.

I decide on a dress to wear for our date tonight and then grab my makeup out of my bag. When I do, the tampons I packed fall out. The tampons I thought I would need but never used.

Hmm. When was I supposed to get my period again?

I grab my phone and check my calendar. Four days ago.

I sit down. I couldn't be.

Could I?

We've used condoms. Every time.

I recall the first night in the dark, us coming together in the hall.

Except for that time.

I shake my head.

I grab my keys, throw on a ball cap and a pair of dark sunglasses, and drive to the nearest pharmacy. I carefully survey the parking lot, making sure there's no one who might take a picture of me in the vicinity. Although, I doubt many paparazzi hang out here.

My hands are shaking as I go in the store. I slip my sunglasses off so I don't look like a complete lunatic, but keep my head down, weaving my way through the store and probably looking like I'm casing the joint. I grab a basket and fill it full of things I don't need, like a jumbo bag of cotton balls and three spiral notebooks, hoping I can hide the pregnancy tests under them. I spy the tests, but don't dare go into the row until I have a plan. I stand a row over and pretend to be looking at condoms, which is slightly ironic.

Once I have memorized which tests I want to buy, I make a quick run through the aisle, stealthily sweeping three different tests into my basket and covering them with the cotton balls.

There's a line of people at the cash register up front, but not one at the pharmacy window, so I decide to go back there. I set the basket on the counter, and keep my head down, pretending to look for my credit card. Thankfully, the woman is nothing but efficient. I suppose pregnancy tests and cotton balls are just an everyday purchase to her, not the life changing one it is for me. She recites the total, I swipe my credit card, sign my name, take my bag, and hightail it out of there.

I sit in the car, feeling sick to my stomach. I take a test out of the bag and stare at it. Think of the implications. Then shove it back in the bag and drive home.

I rush in from the garage and am making my way through the kitchen when Tory says, "Hey, there, what's the rush?"

I stop in my tracks, probably looking like a deer caught in the headlights. "Oh, I just had to run to the store. I think I might be coming down with something."

"Can you come into the office? I have a document for you to sign and want to run a few things by you in regards to your schedule."

"Okay," I try to say calmly, even though my heart feels like it's beating out of my chest. "Let me put this stuff in the bathroom and then I'll be right out."

She grabs a baseball decorated cupcake from the counter, one of two dozen delivered this morning for Pike, and goes back through the breezeway to the office.

"Shit," I say to no one but myself as I take the bag to the bathroom, throw the cotton balls into the closet, and hide the tests underneath them.

I consider taking a quick pee on one of the sticks, going to my office, doing my work, and coming back. But I can't.

What if I'm pregnant?

No, that's crazy. I can't be.

I go to my office and try to pretend things are normal. I am normal. So what if my period is a few days late, and I had unprotected hallway sex with the love of my life? I mean, we've had lots of completely protected sex since then. It's like the law of averages—or, whatever. The odds should be in my favor.

"Okay," Tory says, "Let's talk about your schedule. You have an easy week other than the magazine shoot, then it's crazy busy again. I just got the world-wide premiere schedule from the studio. Frankfurt. Rome. Paris. London. New York. L.A. Six cities in eight days. I've already coordinated everything with your stylist, and we'll have hair and makeup onsite at each location."

She keeps talking and talking. I know it's important stuff, and I should be paying attention, but all I can think about is the fact that I might be pregnant. I glance at the clock. It's four. She'll be working for at least another hour, and I'm supposed to meet Cade at seven. T-minus three hours.

"Do you want me to attend them with you?" she asks.

"Yes, if you can. Premieres always go smoother when you're with me."

"It's really too bad when we go to all these amazing places that we never get time to see them."

"It really is," I agree.

"I'm dying to go back to that spa in Bath," she continues. "It was the most amazing city I've ever been to."

"We should go sometime," I say, appeasing her and trying to get the heck out of here.

"Okay, so the studio will take care of our accommodations. Your stylist is bringing wardrobe options next week. We should be all good, except for the fact that you're acting weird. What's going on?"

"I think maybe I'm coming down with something. Not a big deal, just not feeling great."

"How are things with Cade?"

"Fine."

"When are you going to tell your brother?"

I roll my eyes. "Don't pressure me, okay. I'll tell him when the time is right."

"And when will that be?"

"When I figure things out."

"What's there to figure out?"

"Just stuff, okay!" I say forcefully. "I'm going to lie down."

"Fine," she says with a huff.

I RETURN TO my bedroom and lock the door behind me. Then I go back in the bathroom and dig out the test that claims to be the most sensitive. All of the tests claim to be able to detect a pregnancy within four days of a missed period, but this one says it can detect a pregnancy six days *before*. Since I'm beyond that, I'm hoping it will tell me what I need to know.

I read the instructions, pee on the stick, then set it on a flat surface and watch as the pink color moves across the window. I grab the instructions again, wondering what that means, only to find out it means the test is working.

I look at the timer on my phone.

Two and a half more minutes.

My period has been a few days late before, but it's always shown up. I've never taken a pregnancy test before.

Another *first* since Cade has been back in my life.

I let out a maniacal laugh in spite of my nervousness.

My phone buzzes, causing me to jump.

Okay, this is it.

No, I can't look yet. I grab the instructions and read them one more time. Alright, one pink line means I'm not pregnant. Two pink lines means I am.

But what am I going to do if I am?

I'll tell Cade. He'll either be happy or—I start to cry—not happy. What if he's not happy? What if—just look at the test before you freak out over nothing.

I open my eyes and pick up the stick.

Two pink lines.

Let the freak-out commence.


I RUN THROUGH a gamut of emotions while I'm getting ready for my date. The whole time I was in New York, all I could think about was getting back home to Cade. Especially after all his adorable texts.

Now, I'm dreading our date.

On one hand, I can't wait to see him but, on the other hand, I don't even know how I'm going to carry on a normal conversation! I'll probably burst into tears the second I see him, and he'll wonder what the fuck is wrong with me.

I'm being ridiculous. I'm twenty-eight years old. Cade is thirty-four. It's not like we're kids who got pregnant in the backseat. We're adults. Although I'm nervous about it, I'm excited too. I want children.

My mother will be thrilled.

And Pike will be—pissed.

I GRAB MY handbag and walk out of my room, finding Pike on the couch channel flipping.

"Hey, how was your trip?" he asks.

"Busy," I reply. "How did it go at the doctor's today?"

He pulls a throw off his leg, revealing a full leg cast.

"Oh, wow. I thought you were going to get a boot?"

"Me too. I got royally chewed out for taking off the splints and switching to the boot. I have a hairline fracture on the tibia up by my knee along with all the damage at the ankle. I did get to see the X-rays. Crazy the amount of metal holding it all together. But the good news is no more wheelchair."

"You look happy about that."

He laughs. "*You* should be happy about that. I'm pretty sure I've killed most of your walls with that thing."

"It wasn't that you were a bad driver, per se, it was the fact that your leg was sticking straight out. Made it hard to judge."

Pike smiles at me and pats the sofa, so I sit down next to him.

"I know I've been a pain in the ass. Crabby. Emotional. Probably a bit of a dick. Especially with the whole

Bethany situation. But I just want you to know that I appreciate you taking me in. It means a lot to me."

"Of course I would take you in, Pike. You're my brother. It's what family does. We take care of each other."

He shakes his head, looking emotional. "I just really appreciate it."

"Pike, what else did the doctor say today?"

"What I already knew. That my playing days are probably over."

"Why? You're a pitcher. It's not like you hurt your arm. I read online about a player who broke his ankle, rehabbed, and then had the pins removed so that he could run again. He came back good as new."

"I think I read the same article. The difference is that he was in his early twenties. Not his mid-thirties. And if I do retire, I could take the job as a pitching coach. At first I was sort of offended that they thought I couldn't come back, you know? And I like the idea of being able to stay in the game."

"I like the idea of you being back home," I say. "I've missed not having you around."

"I've missed you, too. Our family is small. Just you, me, and Mom. Maybe it was being in the hospital that made me think a lot about Dad, and I know you're busy, but I'd like it if we spent more time together as a family."

What he says makes me very emotional, causing me

to tear up. "I'd like that too, Pike." I give my brother a big hug.

"Oh, gosh," he says with a laugh. "Don't start crying on me. You know I'm not good with tears."

I laugh at him, grinning and holding his hands across his face.

"So, I've made a decision."

"Are you going to take the job here?"

"No. I'm just going to retire. If I take the coaching job, I'll still be traveling with the team." He gives me a big grin. "Don't laugh, but I'm thinking I might want to settle down. Have some kids or something."

"That's really great, Pike."

"Yeah," he smiles. "You're not getting any younger either, sis. You should start thinking of having kids, too. Wouldn't it be fun if our kids could grow up together?"

"That would be amazing," I reply, stunned, both that my brother wants to settle down and that he chooses today, the day I find out I'm pregnant, to have this conversation.

"You look really pretty. Where are you off to?"

"Dinner. I'll be late though."

"Have fun." He points at the couch he's sitting on. "I'll be here if you need me."

MY MIND IS all over the place during the twenty-minute drive from my house to Cade's. When we first dated, he had a cozy little condo on Laguna Beach, and I lived in my parents' guest house. His commute to work in Beverly Hills sucked, but he could surf every morning and was close to his family and the friends he grew up with.

After we broke up, our careers advanced, and we both relocated, me moving into a cozy ranch in Toluca Lakes—the ideal location when you're filming at the studios in Burbank or at Universal City. Cade bought a condo in Beverly Hills. When I first saw the modern glass and steel structure with its sleek entrance, I expected the condo to be modern and cold, but it wasn't. Even though it's bigger, it still has the same industrial rustic beach vibe of his smaller place and instantly felt familiar.

I put my hand across my belly, still trying to fathom the fact that there is a baby growing inside me. Cade's baby.

I try to figure out what I will say to him. How I could break the news.

I could go serious: *Cade, we need to talk.*

Or take a funny approach: *You'll never guess what happened on the way to the maternity ward.*

The direct approach: Say *I'm pregnant* the second I walk in the door.

The broach a subject approach: *So, Cade, how do you feel about having children?*

The psycho girlfriend approach: Hand him the movie *Knocked Up* and start laughing manically then crying hysterically.

The foodie approach: Put buns in *his* oven.

The sexual approach: Draw a heart and a stick baby on my stomach and wait until he finds it.

The funny sexual approach*: Hey, remember when you put your P in my V and we didn't use a condom? Guess what's in me now?*

The ironic approach: Wrap up the pregnancy test stick, let him open it, and see if he cries like a baby.

The proposal: Ask him to marry me and instead of giving him a ring, give him the pregnancy test.

The surfer approach: *Dude, your life is about to get totally gnarly.*

The casual approach: *Hey, do you know if they make integrated car seats for your Bentley?*

The scarf approach: Chow down on dinner and when he notices the massive intake casually mention that I'm eating for two.

The barf approach: Wait until I have morning sickness, barf all over him, then scream, *It's all your fault!*

The textual approach: Send him a text, telling him I can't come over tonight because I'm sick. When he asks with what, I reply, *Pregnancy.*

The violent approach: Punch him in the face while yelling, *You bastard, you knocked me up!*

The pathetic approach: Burst into tears and sob, hoping he will ask what's wrong.

The indirect approach: Hide a baby rattle in his bathroom and let him find it on his own. Preferably when I'm not there.

The Chinese takeout approach: Stuff a fortune cookie with this message: *Oh, boy, dude, is your life about to change. Like if you want it to. Like if you want to be part of the baby's life. Like we know it was from a crazy, wine-driven screw, but, whatever. Confucius say,* It is what it is.

I shake my head to get all the stupid ideas out. It's not a big deal. You are an adult. It doesn't matter if he wants to play daddy. You will raise the baby yourself if you have to, and you will be an incredible mother.

Possibly.

Shit.

Stop freaking out. Don't even tell him tonight. Give yourself a day or two for this to all soak in, then you will be more level-headed when you break the news.

That's it. That's the plan.

I'll wait.

WHEN I STEP off the elevator, the first thing I notice is the wonderful aroma of tomato sauce mingling with Italian herbs. Cade steps into the entry wearing a pair of jeans, a white dress shirt only half buttoned, and a blue suit jacket, the lapel half flipped up. He looks undone, sexy, and devastatingly handsome. His facial hair is at a three-day scruff. His dark blond hair is pushed back off his face, and all I can think about is running my fingers through it.

With his eyes locked on mine, he takes a step closer, wrapping his arm around my waist and pulling me tightly against him.

"I've missed you," he says, lowering his lips to mine, causing the air to pulse with anticipation. It's only been a couple days since we last kissed, but the simple brush of his lips across mine leaves me aching for him.

I push my fingers through his thick hair. The tantalizingly musky scent of his cologne draws me to his neck. I nuzzle my nose into it then rapidly suck-kiss my way back to his waiting lips and give him a soul-searing kiss.

Our tongues are tangled. Our limbs entwined in a tight embrace. The fire inside me burning out of control.

I feel his arousal pressing against my core as he takes my face in his hands and deepens our kiss. The sound of him kicking the door shut heightens my desire, and I sigh into his mouth when without breaking our kiss, he lifts me up and carries me to his bedroom.

We land roughly on his bed, his tongue deep in my mouth. My fingers slip inside his shirt, feeling the hard planes of his muscled chest.

He abruptly stops kissing me. Stands up. Tosses his jacket to the floor. Undoes his pants, sliding them down just far enough.

"I fucking need you, Palmer," he says, pushing my

skirt up and pulling my panties down with a feral force then flipping me over and pulling me to my knees on the edge of the bed.

He leans forward, his chest pressing against my back, gripping my hips and moving himself into position. I can feel his erection pressing against me and am so turned on I can barely function.

He pushes himself into me in one swift motion, filling me and holding it in place, grinding it inside of me.

"Holy fuck," I mutter out.

"You like that?" he says into my ear. "Tell me you like it if you want me to keep doing it."

"I like it, Cade. Love it," I groan, waves of pleasure pulsing and causing me to tighten around him.

He lets out a devious chuckle and leans back, almost completely pulling out then slapping my ass.

"Do you want me to do that again?" he asks, his voice rough and sexy.

I can't say anything, just mutter a pathetic, "Please."

He responds in the way I want, pushing deep inside me, and making the grinding motion that takes me over the edge. My breathing speeds up, and even though I've orgasmed, I'm aching for more.

"Harder," I manage to whimper, moving my hips back and forth in an attempt to get what I desire.

He curses, adjusts his grip on my hips, and pounds

me roughly with a frenzied abandon. I scream his name, pleasure coursing through me as he's climaxing.

He holds me tightly in place for a few moments, our still bodies a contrast to their motion a moment ago. He leans down and kisses the back of my neck. "I guess I really missed you," he teases as we collapse onto the bed. "These got completely ignored." He moves his hand up to fondle my breasts.

"What's that smell?" I ask, suddenly realizing something is burning.

"Shit!" he yells, leaping off the bed and running to the kitchen. I jump up and follow him.

When I get to the kitchen, he's pulling a loaf of bread out of the oven, the crust black and smoking. He drops the pan in the sink and runs water over it, but the smoke alarm starts beeping anyway.

He shuts the oven door then waves a dishcloth in front of it, causing the beeping to stop.

"Did I make you forget about food, Cade?" I tease.

He pulls me into his arms. "You make me forget about everything."

WE GET DRESSED, then he seats me at a table on his balcony, which I notice he's preset with placemats, china, and even a small bouquet of roses.

"Those are for you," he says, pointing to the flowers. I was supposed to give them to you when you got here."

"They're beautiful," I reply, leaning in to take a whiff. "And they smell wonderful." I watch as he bangs pots around in the kitchen. "Is there anything I can do?"

"Nope, you just sit there and look gorgeous," he says, handing me a glass of wine. I start to take a sip then remember that I'm pregnant.

After a few minutes, he places a big bowl of pasta covered with red sauce in front of us along with a plate of meatballs.

"This is what I've been doing all afternoon."

"You cooked all this?"

"Yep. Mom's recipe."

I look across the table at him and smile, my heart melting into a puddle. "That's really sweet."

"My plan was to feed you before I attacked you," he admits. "But then you had to go and kiss me."

"Oh, so it's my fault?"

His hair is mussed, his eyes bright, his smirk flirtatious. He's downright adorable. "Absolutely."

## Pike

I'M ENJOYING A cold beer and watching the latest on demand big-budget action flick. Although I'm grateful that my sister allowed me to move in with her while I recover, I will admit that it's cramping my style.

I haven't gotten laid in weeks.

I toss back the rest of the beer, pause the movie, and scroll through my phone. Just because the cast is awkward and clunky, doesn't mean my dick doesn't work. And Palmer will be out late.

Hmm.

I decide to text Cameron.

**Me:** *Are you back in town yet? I'm dying to see you.*

I want to say my dick is dying to see her, but I'll throw that into the conversation later.

I take another sip of beer and stare at my phone.

**Cameron:** *Remind me again why we broke up?*
**Me:** *Because you were off doing movies and only flew to my games when you wanted the kind of hot sex your male costars couldn't give you. And we stopped seeing each other because you didn't want a commitment.*
**Cameron:** *We were so young. The first time.*
**Me:** *We weren't so young the second and third times we dated.*
**Cameron:** *We're getting older, Pike.*
**Me:** *I love when you call me that.*
**Cameron:** *Everyone calls you that.*
**Me:** *It always sounds the best coming from you. If I were a girl, I'd say I was swooning.*
**Cameron:** *Bullshit. I literally just landed. I was going*

*to call you tomorrow.*

**Me:** *Come see me.*

**Cameron:** *I'm jetlagged.*

**Me:** *I have a cure for that.*

**Cameron:** *You still rehabbing at Palmer's house?*

**Me:** *I am. But she's out for the night.*

**Cameron:** *I knew I should have shaved my legs this morning.*

**Me:** *I love stubble.*

**Cameron:** *You're just horny.*

I don't reply. She's right. I am. And she knows it. But she also knows that I was in love with her. The first time we dated. The second time we dated. And the third. And pretty much the whole time in between. Cameron has always been the girl who got away. Again and again and again. I rub my palm down my face, not even believing she's coming over.

If there was one girl in my life who made me consider the whole marriage, white picket fence, and having babies thing, it was her. She's fun, sexy, sweet. But god damn is she elusive.

She recently was engaged to a rocker. Everyone thought she was finally ready to settle down. I may have done a little internal cheer when I saw in a tabloid that she broke it off. I tuck my nose under my armpit and take a whiff, making sure that I don't stink. I grab my crutches, hoist myself up off the couch, and go brush my teeth.

ALTHOUGH I'M READY for some rough, dirty fucking, when Cameron arrives, she wants to talk. We've been texting off and on since I got hurt. I was hoping that would be enough.

"How has it been living with your sister?"

"She tries to mother me. But at the same time, I'm really grateful. I needed a lot of help at first. I'm pretty sure my sister is going to need her walls repainted when I leave. I was not a good wheelchair driver."

"And what about your career? The papers say your injury is such that you'll never be back."

I sigh. "The papers might be right."

"Are you giving up on baseball? Retiring?"

"Mentally, I'm not ready to say that yet. But the more time I spend with my sister, the more I realize how much of life I've missed because of baseball."

"You're basically traveling for six months of the year. At first it seems really glamorous, but people don't understand the reality. Sure you travel in a private team plane, and you stay in beautiful hotels, but travel is stressful on your body. The planes, the different beds."

"I opened a bottle of wine for us, but I couldn't carry it in," I tell her, wanting her to relax.

"I'll go get it. Why don't you sit down on the couch and get comfortable."

"You travel a lot for your job," I say.

"Yeah, and it gets old. Sometimes, I want to just stay at my house."

"Do I dare bring up the engagement? Ask what happened?"

She sighs as she's pouring the wine. "Are you on pain medication?"

"Only to sleep," I lie.

She pours me a glass half the size of hers, regardless.

"Cheers," she says clinking my glass and sitting on the couch next to me. She takes a big sip of wine and then walks her fingers down my new cast.

"No one has signed it."

"I just got it today. Don't you think I'm a little old for that?"

"One would think you're a little old to choose the neon green color as well, but there it is," she teases.

"I thought it would cheer me up."

"Did it?"

"Not really."

"Are you all depressed, Pike?"

"First, I was just in pain. Then the realization that my career could be over hit. It's tough to give up something you've worked your whole life for. It'd be like you learning you could never act again."

"That's why I broke off the engagement," she admits, pushing her now blonde hair behind her ear. It looks odd on her.

"Is the hair color for your role?"

"No, I always go crazy and dye my hair after a break-up. I went flaming red after you."

"But you broke up with me."

"Doesn't mean it didn't hurt. It's hard choosing your career over love."

"I'm retiring," I blurt out.

"Really?"

"Really. Just think, I could travel with you and be your sex slave."

"Sex isn't that hard to find, Pike. Love is."

"Cam, you know that I loved you. That I've always—"

"I know, Pike. I know." She leans over and kisses me, avoiding the topic. Honestly, I didn't want her to come over to talk. I wanted her to come over and fuck. But something about her always makes me want more. Her lips are soft and tender. Her hair smells like jasmine. Even though the color is different, she always uses the same shampoo.

My casted leg is up on the sectional's chaise, which makes it hard to twist my body toward her like I should. The cast is like an anchor weighing me down.

"I'm dying to properly kiss you, but I can't fucking move."

She glances at my leg and smiles at me then slides

onto my lap and kisses me.

I feel the rush of excitement I always feel when she gets close to me, especially when she slides her hand down the front of my shorts.

# Palmer

WE CHAT THROUGH dinner, me entertaining him with funny stories from the press junket, like how one of my costars had his black t-shirt turned inside out half the day because he was hung over and had literally rolled out of bed and pulled on whatever clothes were lying on the floor.

Things are going well until he mentions my brother in passing.

And something inside me clicks.

I can't bring a baby into a world where the uncle and father hate each other.

Which means I have to choose.

I'm lost in thought when Cade gets up, takes my hand, and says, "I want to show you something," and leads me to an elevator.

He presses a button, and we emerge on a rooftop terrace with sweeping views of downtown, romantically lit with lanterns. It reminds me of our first date and the night we got engaged.

"It's gorgeous up here," I say. "And the views are incredible." I turn in a circle taking it all in.

Cade takes my hand, leading me to the center of the circle of lanterns.

Oh, no. Is he going to propose? Now?

I start to panic. My mind racing. My heart feeling like it's beating out of my chest.

No. No. No.

"Palmer," he says, dropping to one knee.

"I'm sorry," I cry out, then I turn and race toward the elevator.

I'M SOBBING BY the time I reach my car. Cade shouts from behind me, telling me to stop.

But I don't.

I get in my car, quickly start it, and drive away.

My heart hurts. Tears are blurring my vision—much like they did when I broke up with him six years ago.

*I drive home in a flurry of tears, barely paying attention to where I'm going. I'm so mad I can hardly see straight.*

*And I'm sobbing.*

*How could Cade, the man who is supposed to love me unconditionally do this to me? This is my big break! And he was willing to jeopardize it just because he didn't want me to do a sex scene? No matter how much I love him, I can't marry someone who doesn't support my career.*

*I bawl and slam my hand on the steering wheel.*

*A car behind me honks, letting me know that a light has turned green. I look up to see where I even am.*

*My hands are shaking, my whole body shaking, as I try to make it home.*

*When I finally get to my parents' house, where I'm living in the guest house, I completely break down, leaning my head against the steering wheel and letting it all out.*

*I was supposed to come here with Cade to tell Mom and Pike the good news, but now—*

*Now, I just—*

*I don't even know what to do.*

*I get out of my car, slamming the door with way too much force, as my brother pulls into the driveway.*

*"What's wrong?" he asks, immediately looking worried. "Is Mom okay?"*

*I can't say anything. I just sob some more.*

# *Pike*

CAMERON IS BOUNCING up and down on my dick in the middle of what's been an all-night fuck fest.

The back door opens with a bang, my sister walks into the room, and yells, "You've got to be fucking kidding me!" Then marches off to her room.

"Shit," I say as Cameron jumps off me.

Then she starts giggling.

"It's been a long time since I got caught having sex. Remember that time on the beach in Miami? I hadn't seen you in two weeks and was so fucking horny I could barely stand it."

I laugh, too. "Those were the good old days."

She slips back into her clothes. "I thought tonight was pretty damn good, but that's besides the point. We need to check on your sister. She looked really upset."

"I suppose so, since she just caught me with my dick in you."

"No, I mean she had mascara running down her face, like she'd been crying."

"Really? I didn't notice."

"Why don't you get dressed, and I'll go check on her."

She goes down the hall and knocks on my sister's door. "Hey, Palmer, sorry about that. I'm headed out. Um, it's hard for him to get around. Thus, the couch."

I hear the door squeak open. Cameron asks my sister if she's okay. Palmer replies with a sob.

When Cameron escorts her out to the family room, she's got her arm wrapped tightly around her, making it look like she's holding her up.

"What's wrong?" I ask as she sits in a chair across from me. "You haven't looked like that since the day you and Cade broke up. Do I need to go kick someone's ass again? Mop up?" As soon as it comes out of my mouth, I realize it was a mistake to bring up the past. Must be the meds, the wine, and having Cameron on top of me. My mind is not fully functioning.

"Cade was going to propose," she stutters out between crying, which causes Cameron to stop in her tracks.

"To who?"

"To me." Instead of leaving as promised, Cameron returns to the couch and takes my sister's hand.

"Why?"

"Because we're in love. We got back together in Tahoe, and I've been seeing him since."

I'm immediately pissed. "Why would you do that? He broke your heart."

"I got over it. You should, too."

"Are you fucking kidding me?" I say, not even able to believe this is coming out of my sister's mouth. "How could you be so stupid after what he did to you? How could you ever trust him again? You're an idiot if you think he's going to change for you. Once a cheater, always a cheater."

Her face twists and she stands up and yells at me. "Don't you dare say that! Ever! Cade would *never* cheat on me!"

"What are you talking about?" I ask her, confused. "He already did. That's why you broke up!"

Her eyes get big. "What are you talking about? That's not why we broke up!"

She buries her face in her hands and starts bawling again.

"Tell me what happened between you and Cade!"

She shakes her head. "I can't. You'll hate me."

"Palmer Alexis Montlake, you better fucking tell me what happened."

"Sideboob, Pike. We broke up because of a sideboob."

"I don't understand."

"We got into a fight over the nudity clause in a contract."

"But you told me he cheated on you," I say, trying to understand. "I beat him up because he cheated on you."

"No, Pike, I didn't say that. I would have *never* said that."

"What did you say then?"

"I don't remember what I said. I was pretty hysterical, but I know I never would have said that! But I also didn't want to tell you the real reason. I didn't need you lecturing me, too." She stands up. "And I don't need you lecturing me now! He was going to propose again tonight, and I ran out!"

"Again?" both Cameron and I say.

"What the hell? When were you engaged?"

She wipes the back of her hand across her face in an

attempt to dry her tears. "We got engaged two days before we broke up. He recreated our first date, took me to the top of a mountain where there were lanterns and a table set for two. It was so romantic, and I loved him so deeply."

"Why the fuck didn't you tell me?"

"We were going to tell you and Mom the night we broke up."

"That's not what I'm talking about. If you got engaged, you had been dating for a while. Behind my back. Why?"

"Look at your body language right now, Pike. Your fists are balled up, your chest puffed out, ready to whip someone's ass. Cade wanted to tell you. I wouldn't let him until I knew it was serious. Then Dad died. And I couldn't do it. Couldn't cause our family any more heartache." She stands up. "I'm going to bed. I'm sorry for interrupting your night," she says to Cameron before marching toward her room.

"Wait," Cameron yells. "If he makes you so happy, you got back together, and he was going to propose, why are you home crying instead of happily celebrating?"

"Because I would have had to say no, and I couldn't bear to see the look on his face when I did," she says, slamming her bedroom door behind her.

"YOU CALLED HIM an asshole," Cameron says to me. "I

thought when he carried you out on the field that meant you two finally made up."

I shake my head. "No, we didn't even talk. All the networks wanted us to be interviewed together, but he wouldn't. He hates me."

"Sounds like maybe you were wrong about him."

"I just don't get it, Cam. When I went to the bar that night, he didn't deny anything."

"Did you accuse him of cheating?"

"I don't even remember what I said, I was so pissed. I think it was something about seeing my sister behind my back and fucking with her heart."

"You should call him," she says, handing me my phone.

"I can't. I deleted his number after I beat the shit out of him. It was weird. I accused him. Punched him. He took it. Barely fought back. Now I understand why."

"I think you owe him a long overdue apology."

"If she loves him, why would she have said no?"

"Too soon, maybe? When was Tahoe?"

"A couple weeks ago."

"That's a pretty quick proposal. That'd be like us getting back together tonight and then in a couple weeks you ask me to marry you."

I scratch my eyebrow. "That's one thing Cade and I had in common. When we knew something was right, we went for it. We didn't take no for an answer. Neither one of us ever have." I reach out and touch Cameron's face gently. "What would you say?" I ask her, partially for some insight on my sister, and partly because I wonder if in some luck-filled world she would ever say yes.

"If I felt it was too soon, I would have told you so. But I wouldn't have run out on you. I wouldn't be sitting in my room bawling my eyes out."

"Putting yourself out there so soon like he did—that takes a lot of guts," I admit.

"You admire him, don't you?"

"He was my best friend, Cam. Would still be to this day if it weren't for my sister."

"Maybe the reason she had to say no to him isn't about them, Pike. Maybe it's about *you*."

AFTER CAMERON TUCKS me in and gives me a good-night kiss, I lay in bed for hours, trying to remember that day. But all I can remember is the way I felt—pissed, hurt, and betrayed. I can still recall the way I felt, but not what was said.

At some point, I drift off to sleep.

*I'm back in town and headed over to Mom's house for dinner.*

*When I pull in the drive, Palmer is just getting out of her car. I watch as she slams the door shut and turns toward me.*

*I instantly know something is wrong. I throw the car into park and jump out.*

*"What's wrong? Is Mom okay?"*

*Palmer doesn't say anything, just sobs. I put my hand on her shoulder. "Palmer, tell me what's wrong! Are you okay?"*

*"Do I look okay?" she yells back at me. "Because I'm not. I'm horrible. And so incredibly hurt. My heart hurts, Pike."*

*"What happened?"*

*"Cade," she blubbers out between sobs.*

*"What did he do?"*

*"We've been dating—" she says.*

*"Why didn't he tell me?" I ask, but I already know. That chicken shit bastard.*

*"And then Dad died," she whimpers and drops to her knees. She's so filled with hurt she can't even stand.*

*I drop to the ground and pull her into a hug. "I miss Dad, too," I say gently, knowing I need to tread lightly when she's this upset. But I have to know. I have to fucking know what he did before I fucking kill him. "It'll all be okay. Tell me what happened."*

*"I thought I could trust him, but I can't," she says hysterically.*

I wake up with a start, her words still echoing in my head.

*"I thought I could trust him, but I can't."*

She was right. She never said he cheated on her. I just assumed.

I was wrong.

And I can't wait any longer.

I grab my phone and text Carter, asking him for Cade's number.

He replies with it even though it's three in the morning.

I hit the number before I lose my nerve.

I owe my friend an apology.

# November 16th
## *Palmer*

MY FACE IS plastered to my pillow when I wake up. I don't know what time it was when I finally cried myself to sleep last night.

I get up, needing to pee. I start to sit on the toilet, but see the pregnancy test I took last night still lying on the back of the stool. I check it and see that the double pink lines are still there.

I pull the package it came in out of the trash and reread it.

*False negatives can happen if the pregnancy hormone isn't strong enough yet. False positives are rare.*

I throw open the linen closet and grab the other two tests I bought yesterday. There's one of each brand.

Maybe they will turn negative. Maybe the positive was just a rare fluke.

But as I hold my stomach and rock back and forth, I don't wish for that. I want a baby. And to be pregnant with Cade's baby is everything I've ever dreamed of. As a young girl, I crushed on him. As a young woman, I loved him with everything I had. But now, I just feel jaded.

And tired.

I pull the packages open, read the directions for each, pee into a cup, dip each stick into the cup, and then sit on the edge of the tub and wait—crying both happy and sad tears, when each test turns positive.

Wrapping a thick robe around me for comfort, I pad out to my kitchen in search of a cup of coffee.

## *Pike*

I'M LEANING ON my crutches in the kitchen, waiting for my toast to brown, when my sister walks in.

"I remembered what you said to me that night," I tell her. "You said you thought you could trust him but couldn't. You were so upset you could barely stand. I assumed you found him with another woman."

"I got picked for the lead in a romantic comedy. Cade mentioned it was practically a done deal, that he just had to negotiate a nudity clause. It was my big break. I couldn't believe he would risk losing the opportunity because they wanted me to do a sex scene where I showed a little boob. I trusted Cade completely—as my agent and as my love. I accused him of just being jealous." Tears form in her eyes. She stops speaking to brush them away. "We had just gotten engaged. I was the happiest I had ever been."

"But, I thought—all this time—that he cheated on you."

"I didn't know you thought that, Pike, or I would have set the record straight. I thought you were mad at him because we dated and didn't tell you. You went and beat him up and then came home and told me that he'd never bother me again. Of course, that wasn't what I wanted. I just wanted to do the movie."

"There's something I need to tell you, Palmer. Something you need to know."

"What?" she asks.

"I think it's all my fault," I admit. "I made him promise."

"Promise what?"

"When he became your agent, I made him promise to take care of my little sister. To not let her get taken advantage of. I told him our family trusted him. I trusted him. He didn't want to represent you—said mixing business and friendship was a recipe for disaster. What if you wanted to be naked in a movie? I made him promise he would never let you. Not long after Dad died, he came to me and explained how nudity clauses work. How as you were getting more famous, it would come up. How it could be done tastefully. I got really pissed. Told him our dad would roll over in his grave if that ever happened. I think that's why he was so against it. Why he fought you on it. Because he was being my friend."

"*That's* why he was so adamant? Because of his promise to you?"

"I think so. He was trying to juggle our friendship, your relationship, and your career. That had to have been tough for him. And then I thought he cheated on you, so I went and beat the shit out of him. He never told me. I completely ruined our friendship."

"You said he ruined it when he started dating me."

"Do you still love him, Palmer?" I ask her, knowing that's all that matters at this point. I want my sister to be happy.

"Yes."

"I don't understand, though. You've never appeared nude in any movie."

"I know. I broke up with him over it, but I couldn't do it. And then I couldn't admit to him that I was wrong."

"He was . . . my best friend."

She buries her face in her hands.

"Palmer, it'll be okay. Just call Cade and tell him everything. Sort it all out."

"I can't just *call* him, Pike!" She bursts out sobbing. "Because I'm pregnant!"

"You're *what?* Whose baby is it?"

She lets out a frustrated and pathetic sounding sigh. "It's Cade's."

"Is that why he was going to propose, because you're pregnant?"

"He has no idea. I just did the test yesterday before I went out. It was positive. I was freaking out. On the drive over, I was trying to figure out how to tell him. Then I decided I'd wait. Let myself get used to the idea first. We had an amazing dinner that he cooked for me at his place then he showed me his rooftop patio. It was gorgeous and I was mesmerized by the view."

"Then what happened?" I ask, trying to drag the story out of her.

"There were all these lanterns. And he dropped to one knee. I knew he was going to propose. I freaked out. Ran away. Drove home."

I hobble over, using the counter to support my weight instead of a crutch, and wrap an arm around her, just like I used to when she was little. I was never one of those mean older brothers who taunted or made fun of her. We've always been close despite our six-year age difference. I have always been her big brother and protector, and I realize I have completely fucked up those duties.

"It'll be okay, Peaches," I say.

"I'm not sure how it could be. You should have seen

the look on Cade's face. And it was so beautiful."

"Why didn't you want to tell me? We were always so close. I just wanted you to be happy."

"That's not true, Pike. You were always telling your friends that I was off-limits. That I was young. That they couldn't even look. Remember when Cade came with us to Tahoe for a week and then all your friends were coming up to celebrate his twenty-first birthday?"

"Yeah."

"I snuck into his room. Into his bed."

"You did what? You were like twelve."

"I was fifteen, Pike. I'd been modeling. Traveling internationally. I didn't feel fifteen, but I was still a virgin. I wanted Cade to be my first. I'd always crushed on him."

"And what happened?"

"He turned me down. Gently."

"He's always been a good man, hasn't he? Even back in school when we were mowing through women, he always treated them with respect. It's why I was so adamant about him being your agent. I trusted him implicitly. So how did you get together?"

"When I signed with him, I was nineteen. I'd been around by then. Rock stars, movie stars, male models. None of them made me heat up the way Cade did every time he walked into a room. I hit on him again. He said he couldn't date clients. I told him I wanted to cancel our agreement. He told me that I needed him. But the way he looked at me when we were together, it gave me confidence. I knew eventually it would happen."

"When did it?"

"My twenty-first birthday. I pretty much offered my drunk self up to him on a silver platter. He took me home. I was in heaven. I was traveling a lot, suggested we keep it casual. Wouldn't let him tell anyone. He finally gave me an ultimatum. We date or we stop hooking up. He said I meant too much to him. I said let's date and see what happens, but I still wouldn't let him tell you. He took me on a first date, and what a first date it was. We helicoptered to a snowmobile lodge for a moonlight ride. But when we got to the top of the mountain, there were all these lanterns set up and a candlelit dinner just for us. It was amazing. He was amazing. And then Dad died. I told him I couldn't deal with it. When he brought it up a few months later, I told him I wouldn't tell you until I knew for sure he was serious. So he proved it to me by proposing. I'm so ashamed."

"Why?"

"Because I never told Dad about Cade. He loved him like a son, and he would have been happy that we were together."

"He would have been happy if you were happy. Same for me."

"I don't think that's true. You would have been mad

at him for getting with your little sister. Tell me that you wouldn't have taken it as a betrayal."

I sigh. "You're probably right. It would have taken me a while to get used to it. It's a guy code thing. You don't mess with your best friend's little sister."

"See exactly."

I point a finger at her. "Unless . . ."

"Unless what?"

"Unless, you're serious about her. Then it's about being a good man for her. Taking care of her. It's a completely different thing."

"Then you've mellowed with age. So what's up with you and Cameron?"

"I'm not a good man. I wouldn't want you with someone like me."

"You are too a good man."

"Man, maybe. Boyfriend. Husband. Anything with a commitment, not so much."

"You travel all the time. That's hard."

"Plenty of the guys on the team are happily married. They have kids. They make it work. I've never wanted to make it work."

"Except with Cameron?"

"Yeah, I guess."

"So why don't you do something about it?"

"Look at me. I'm done. My career is over."

"You've earned a lot of money. You've saved most of

it. You don't need to work ever again."

"But that's what you don't get. What people who aren't in it don't get. It's *all* I've ever worked for. And to have it taken away like that, it's hard to deal with, emotionally. Mentally. I've been a ballplayer my whole life. It's who I am."

"But it shouldn't define you. It's your job, not your life. At least it shouldn't be."

"None of that matters right now. When are you going to tell Cade about the baby?"

Her phone buzzes with a text. I read it.

**Cade:** *I don't know what to say, Palmer. I must have misread things between us. Please call me.*

She closes her eyes and shakes her head. "You're not the only stubborn ass in the family."

"But I still don't understand. If you're happy with him, why did you run out? Why haven't you answered his calls? I've heard your house phone ringing all morning."

"If you knew he was calling, and the phone was sitting right next to you, why didn't *you* answer it?"

"Because—"

"Yeah, exactly."

"Because he wasn't calling for me."

"I ran out last night because you and mom are the only family I have left. And I can't marry a man you hate. So I'm just going to raise the baby alone."

She walks away.

I hobble over to the kitchen table and sit down, absorbing everything she told me.

I understand why Cade proposed back then. Palmer needed him to prove to her that their relationship was worth it.

Cameron was right. This isn't about her and Cade anymore. It's about me and Cade.

I can't just talk about it. I can't tell her what she should or shouldn't do. I have to prove it to her.

I try calling Cade again, but he doesn't answer. If he doesn't answer my calls, it's going to be difficult to talk to him.

So I call someone else, make a few arrangements, and then hang up.

If I'm going to be an uncle, I'd better get my shit together.

# Cade

I DIDN'T SLEEP much last night. Mostly tossed and turned. Relived last night over and over in my head, trying to figure out where it went wrong. How I misread things.

I make myself some breakfast then poke around on

the computer to kill time before I meet my trainer.

I check my phone for the thousandth time since last night to see if I have a missed call or text from her.

I don't.

But I do have a few missed calls from an unknown number. Probably another reporter. You'd think they'd give it a rest.

I press play to listen to the message anyway. Anything to take my mind off her.

*Hey, it's Pike. Um, so, could we maybe get together? Talk?*

Fuck that. I don't need to get my ass kicked by her brother. Her running off last night kicked it enough.

Shaking my head, I head to the gym. Carter and I meet most mornings, working with the same personal trainer, and they get pissy when I'm late.

He's not here when I arrive, so trainer Tom waits a few minutes then decides to punish me with squats.

Carter strolls in dressed in a suit and without his gym bag.

"You not working out today?" Tom asks him.

"Tom, could I speak to you for a moment in private?"

I wonder what the fuck is up, but I can't deal with any possible brother drama right now, so I continue my punishment, pushing my body until my muscles start shaking.

"Cade," the same voice from the message says to me.

I turn around and see Pike, my former best friend, confidante, and teammate, hobbling into the room on crutches while my traitorous brother holds the door for him. Pike looks rough. We've both had a lot of injuries over the years, but I've heard the news. This one is different. This one will probably end his career. And more than likely he knows I've been seeing his sister again. Otherwise, he wouldn't be here.

I flash a glare in my brother's direction.

"Just hear him out," Carter says, quickly exiting the room and shutting the door tightly behind him.

"Chicken shit," I mutter under my breath.

Pike doesn't move, just stands by the door, leaning on his crutches.

"Why are you here?" I ask him.

"Because I owe you an apology."

I sit down on an exercise ball, mostly from the shock of it. That wasn't what I expected him to say.

"That's good," I joke. "I'd hate to have to whoop on a guy with a cast."

We stare at each other in an awkward silence. Pike seemingly lost in thought.

Finally, he says, "Look, this isn't about me. It's about Palmer and her happiness."

"So you know we've been seeing each other again?"

He nods. "I do."

"So why are you here?"

"When you and I stopped being friends—when I punched you—it was because I got some incorrect information."

"I don't understand."

"I thought you cheated on her."

"What? I *never* would have cheated on her. I was in love with her! I fucking proposed!"

"You've always loved her, haven't you?" he asks softly.

No point in trying to deny it now. "Yes, I'm in love with your sister. I have been since she was fifteen. But I waited six excruciatingly long years before I acted on it, because I knew you would see it as a betrayal."

"I just want my sister to be happy."

"That's all I want, too."

"She came home upset last night."

"I was pretty upset myself. She won't return my calls. I'm not sure what to do." I run my hand through my hair in frustration. All these years, he thought I cheated on her? No wonder he beat the shit out of me. I would have done the same.

"Fight for her."

"I thought you said you owed me an apology?"

"I do. I'm sorry I reacted the way I did. You were my best friend. I owed you the chance to explain."

I nod, accepting it. It's all I need to hear.

"How's the leg?" I ask.

"Fucked."

"How are you taking that?"

"I'm living with my sister and can barely stand and pee by myself. How do you think I'm doing?"

"Do you know why she ran off last night? Did she tell you anything?"

"Yeah, I know why. Because she can't marry someone her brother hates."

"Meaning it's on you."

"Yeah."

"And how do you feel about that?"

"Well, *Mom's* always liked you," he says with a grin.

I stand up, take a few steps toward him, and hold out my hand to shake his, glad this is behind us.

"Screw that, bro," he says, throwing a fisted arm around me in a man hug. "Now, what are you going to do about my sister?"

# November 17th
## *Palmer*

I MOPED AROUND the house all day yesterday, crushed by my actions, but knowing I did the right thing. I honestly thought that Cade would text me, call me, come over—something. But other than his text the other night, I haven't heard from him.

Thank goodness I didn't let him propose or tell him about the baby. It's obvious now that it was just about the sex. Old feelings I thought were still there because the sex was so amazing.

I open my eyes and focus on the script changes in front of me. I've got to approve them and get them back to the production company today.

"Hey," Tory says from her desk directly across the room. "Ashlyn Roberts and I just had the most lovely conversation. She really is delightful."

"Yeah, she's a sweet girl."

"She said she tried to call you, but you didn't answer."

I look down at my cell and see I missed her call. "I

didn't hear it vibrate, I guess." I point at the script. "Trying to get this done."

"She wants to invite you to dinner tonight. We got to talking, and she invited me, too. I think we should go. It will be fun."

"I've got too much to do," I reply, putting my head back down to continue my work.

Cameron wanders into the office. "Hey, I just talked to Ashlyn. She said she invited you all for dinner, too." Cameron has become a permanent fixture at my house, it seems.

"What's the dinner for?" I ask.

"She has a new house and wants to show it off. Cash has something work-related to do tonight, so she thought a girls' night was in order."

Pike hasn't said much to me since I told him I'm pregnant. I thought he'd lecture me about it, but he's hasn't, seemingly giving me the space I need.

Or it could be because I locked myself in my room all day yesterday.

"I didn't know you two were friends," I say to Cameron.

"Is it because I'm old?" she laughs. "Just kidding. Ashlyn and I did those 'beauty at every age' makeup ads together, where they highlighted every decade. She was twenties, and I was thirties. We had a blast together."

I nod my head, thinking it through. I like Ashlyn a

lot. Yes, she's now Cade's sister-in-law, but if Cash is out, and she's inviting girls over, it's not like Cade would be there. It might be good for me to get out of the house.

"We'd need to leave the house shortly," Tory says to me. "What do you want to do?"

I make a snap decision. What the hell. "Let's do it."

"Um," Cameron says, scrunching up her nose at me. "You might wanna go change."

I look down at the yoga pants and T-shirt I put on when I got home from Cade's the other night. I wore them to bed, kept them on all day yesterday, and repeated last night. I didn't bother to change when I came to work this morning. I just put my hair into a messy bun and then walked across the courtyard to the guest house I turned into my office. Honestly, I'm not sure if I even brushed my teeth. I've just been going through the motions.

"Yeah, I probably should," I agree.

THE SHOWER WATER running over me is not only cleansing my body, but it's purifying my mind. When I emerge, I feel better.

I look in the mirror at my naked body and study it. Other than a teeny bruise where Cade gripped my hip the other night, it looks completely normal. My boobs don't look bigger. My stomach is still flat. I'm certainly not glowing.

I blow out my hair too quickly, which causes it to look frizzy, so I throw it into a messy braid. I focus on doing my makeup carefully—doing it so that I look naturally beautiful even though I'm wearing a lot of makeup. My makeup artist always says the key is blending and contouring. Ashlyn loves to take pictures, and I don't want Cade to see a photo of me looking anything other than amazing.

After my makeup is done, I realize that I look like I did the night of my first party as a Hollywood actress. The night I stopped by Cade's office all done up, hoping his plea for me stop by and sign a contract late at night was just a ruse to get me there so he could seduce me. I was disappointed when he actually had a contract waiting.

I dig through my closet and pull out the pink bandage dress he said he fantasized about, hoping it still fits right. I pull it on and take a look in the full-length mirror, adjust my boobs in my push-up bra to give me more cleavage, and throw on silver heels.

I don't know why, but this dress makes me feel like a powerful woman who is in control of her life, and it improves my mood.

When I meet up with Cameron and Tory in the kitchen, Cameron lets out a whistle. "Damn, girl. You've got it going on. It's too bad I like dick."

Tory bursts out laughing. "You and me both."

"I'm glad Cameron likes dick, too," Pike chuckles, causing the girls to giggle.

"Is it too much?" I ask.

"No," Pike says from the couch. "You look beautiful. I called a car for you girls, and it's waiting out front. Have fun."

Cameron leans over the back of the couch and gives him a steamy good-bye kiss. "You're the best," she says, mussing his hair.

## *Pike*

As SOON AS the girls leave, I throw the blanket off me, grab my crutches, and peek out the front door. After watching the car pull away, I text Carter. A few moments later, he pulls into the driveway, and I hop in the car with him.

My mom leans up from the backseat and gives me a kiss on the cheek.

"This is so exciting," she says.

# *Palmer*

"WOW, THIS HOUSE is amazing," Tory says as we pull through the gates and Cash and Ashlyn's new home comes into view.

"As high up as it is, I bet it has an amazing view," Cameron adds.

"I can't wait to see the inside," Tory agrees.

Ashlyn is at the door waiting for us and greets us with hugs. "You'll have to humor me and take the grand tour first. I'm still in shock I even live here."

"It's beautiful," Tory gushes, noting the intricacy of the beamed ceilings and the iron stair railings.

As we walk into the kitchen and great room, Cameron points out the windows at the Pacific Ocean and says, "What a view!"

Ashlyn takes us outside and shows us expansive grounds with a pool, spa, fire pit, and garden.

As we move to the second floor from one amazing room to the next, Cameron says, "I just have to ask who your decorator is. I need to redo my house in Hawaii, and I love how soft and pretty it is."

"Cash bought the house without telling me and brought me here on our wedding night. It was his gift to me. Crazy. It's my total dream house, and somehow he knew. His mom worked with her designer to choose everything. Wait until you see the nursery."

"The nursery?" I gulp. "Are you pregnant?"

"Oh, gosh no," she says with a laugh. "Cash and I aren't ready for that, but his mother certainly is." She stops in front of a room and opens the door.

I walk into the nursery, tears building. It takes everything I have to hold it together. It's beautiful.

"The wallpaper is sheet music for the lullaby Cash's mother used to sing all the kids to sleep to," Ashlyn tells us, hugging herself.

"It's so perfect," Cameron says. "The soft walls, the oriental rug, the rich velvet draperies."

"And the chandelier," Tory says. "Love the chandelier."

"It's opulent and beautiful, but the fabric patterns are so playful. Now I want to have a baby," Cameron laughs. "Just so I can have a room like this."

Ashlyn laughs too, the sound of it ebbing and fading. A warm sensation envelops me.

"Are you feeling okay?" Tory asks me, touching my shoulder. "You look white as a ghost."

I grab the crib for support, feeling dizzy like I could pass out. "I think maybe I'm a little dehydrated."

"Well, let's go back down to the kitchen and get everyone something to drink," Ashlyn says happily.

I follow everyone down the steps and into the great room.

As the girls in front of me peel out of line, I see that

we're not alone.

Cade is standing in the center of the room with Pike next to him, grins on both their faces. They look happy, like they used to look on the ball field after winning another game. My mother is standing next to Cade's parents, and Cash, Carter, and Chloe are flanking them.

I don't understand. What are Cade and Pike doing standing next to each other?

Ashlyn hands me a glass of water, and I slurp it down greedily.

"What are you all doing here?" I stutter out.

Pike steps toward me. "I apologized to Cade. Told him that I misunderstood you and thought he had cheated on you. He understands now why I had to beat the shit out of him. We're all good."

Cade takes two strides toward me. I'm frozen, not sure what to do.

"Last night, I was going to ask you to marry me."

"I know. That's why I had to leave."

"I screwed up though, just like I did the first time. Tonight I want to fix that."

"What do you mean?"

"When I asked you to marry me the first time, I didn't ask your family for your hand in marriage like I should have. I never should have listened to you when you said you didn't want to tell our families until the time was right. It's something I regret to this day. And I should have manned up and asked your brother before the other night—even though he probably would have said no. So, I'm doing it right this time. You just had me under your spell back then, and all I wanted was to make you happy. But it's not just about you. It's about us. It's about the guy who was my best friend. It's about our mothers who have secretly stayed friends all these years."

Cade walks over to my mother, takes her hand, and leads her over to Pike. He looks him in the eye, man-to-man. "As the man of the house, do you give me your blessing to marry your sister? I promise to be faithful to her, to love her always, and to take care of her."

Pike gets teary, slaps him on the back, and nods his head. "Yeah, man, I do."

Cade turns to my mom. "Mrs. Montlake, can you give me your blessing? Do you think your husband would have approved?"

Mom hugs him tightly as tears stream down her face. "He would have wholeheartedly approved. As do I."

"What about you, Mom? Dad?" Cade says to his parents. "What do you think? Should I ask her to marry me?"

"Third time's a charm, Cade," his mom replies.

"Just ask her already!" Cash and Chloe yell out.

Cade struts toward me, and I know what's about to happen.

And I can't let it.

# *Cade*

WHILE EVERYONE AROUND us looks happy, Palmer looks like she's about to pass out.

Not the reaction I was hoping for.

Damn if I didn't about die when I saw her walk into this room, wearing the dress of many fantasies. I took it as divine sign.

But now I'm not so sure.

"Uh, if everyone could wait a second," she says, her eyes darting around the room in panic. "I need to talk to Cade in private, please." She grabs me by the arm and drags me out to the patio.

"You do know I was about to propose, right? And that you just interrupted it?"

"I know, Cade. It's just that I need to tell you something important before you do. Something that might affect your decision. Something that could change your mind about me."

"Are you a lesbian?" I ask.

"No," she says, crinkling up her adorable nose.

"Are you a criminal?"

"No, but—"

"Do you love me?" I ask, taking her into my arms.

"Yes, Cade, I do."

"That's all that really matters then." I hold my hands out like it's a done deal.

She grabs my face, her hands holding my cheeks tight, forcing me to look straight into her eyes. "Cade, I'm pregnant."

Her words take my breath away. I don't know what I expected her to say, but that was not it.

"You're what?" I ask. "Are you serious?"

"Yes, Cade. I am. I knew you were going to propose last night. I took the pregnancy test right before I went to your house." Her eyes fill with tears. "And I just couldn't. Not when you and Pike were—"

"Pike and I are fine now."

"But I'm not. I'm pregnant, and I know that changes things, and I don't want you to be with me just because of that. I don't want you to marry me because of that."

"I didn't know you were pregnant, Palmer. I want to marry you because I love you. But you're right. This does change things." I put my head down, taking it in. Palmer is pregnant.

"Cade, I—"

I grab her face and kiss her.

"You need to just shut up for a second and let me process this." I stare into the eyes of the woman I love. The woman who is carrying my baby.

"But, Cade—"

I lean forward and kiss her again, shutting her up.

"Palmer, I don't think I've heard anything in my life that's ever made me this happy."

I look at where we're standing, on a stone-paved terrace perched high above the ocean. A different view than the first time I proposed, but like the planned roof-top proposal, we're still up high. That's how I always feel when I'm with her. High. Like I'm soaring through the clouds. Like nothing can stop me. This isn't how I planned to do it, but nothing with her has gone according to plan.

But it feels right.

"Palmer, I've been in love with you since you were fifteen. Not even a curling iron to the head could stop me. I've never felt happier in my life than I do in this moment. I love you so much, and knowing that you're pregnant with my baby makes this that much sweeter." I drop to one knee, take her hand, and gaze into her eyes. "No fancy words this time. No poems or fanfare. Just three important things. I *love* you. I *need* you in my life. I *want* you to be my wife. Palmer, will you marry me?"

She wraps her arms around me in a hug as I stand up. She's nodding and crying, but still hasn't said yes.

And that makes me nervous. Is she crying because she's happy?

I decide to use the jewelry to try and seal the deal. I hold up the engagement ring I gave her six years ago.

"That's my ring!" she says excitedly through her tears. "I can't believe you didn't hock it."

"I could never do that." I take her right hand in mine

and gently slip it onto her finger.

She laughs. "It's supposed to go on the other hand, Cade."

"This ring represents our past. The love I've always had for you." I reach in my pocket, pull out a black velvet box, and open it.

"Oh, my god, Cade. It's beautiful!"

"You can't have this one until you say yes."

She glances up at me, one innocent look speaking volumes about our happiness to come. "Are you sure?"

"Absolutely."

"Then the answer is yes, Cade. I can't wait to marry you." This time I take her left hand and slide the ring on it. "It's twice the size of the first one."

"That's because I waited twice as long as I wanted." I brush my lips against hers as our families start cheering from inside the house.

"Does anyone else know?" I ask her. "About the baby?"

"Just you and Pike," she says.

"Let's go tell everyone we're engaged, but let's keep the other news a secret for a little while longer."

# December 26th
## *Palmer*

A MONTH LATER, on the day after Christmas, our families are gathered in Tahoe for our wedding.

I can't imagine a more perfect place to start our life together.

I slide into my gorgeous, blush-colored gown and Tory zips me up.

"Amazing," she says.

"It's time," Pike says, knocking gently on the door of one of the upstairs bedrooms where I've been getting ready. "Are you decent?"

"Yes, come in."

Pike opens the door and sees me in my dress for the first time. "You look stunning. I can't believe my baby sister is getting married."

"You look pretty spiffy yourself. Do you think Cade will like my dress?"

"Cade loves you. Of course, he's going to love your dress." He gives my hand a squeeze and then I follow him out to the catwalk overlooking the two-story great room of Cade's new house. *Our* house. It looks beautiful. He and his brothers spent the afternoon hanging twinkle lights in rows across the ceiling. The fireplace mantel is decorated in ivory, blush, and gold. And Cade is standing in front of it looking so incredibly handsome that I can't wait to get down there and marry him.

"I wish Dad could be here to walk you down the aisle," Pike says. "He'd be so proud of you, Palmer."

"You're going to make me cry," I tell him, wiping little tears from the corner of my eyes, trying not to ruin my makeup. I want to look perfect when Cade sees me for the first time.

"Honestly, Pike, I think he'd be more proud of you. I can't tell you how happy I am that you and Cade are friends again."

"Screw friends, Palmer, he says with a grin. "Thanks to you, we're going to be brothers." He gives me a kiss on the cheek. "I'll meet you at the bottom."

He gets in the elevator and takes it down to the main floor. He's going to walk me down the aisle, crutches and all, but we didn't want to risk the stairs. He announced his retirement from baseball a few weeks ago and is planning to propose to Cameron, here, on New Year's Eve. We aren't going on a honeymoon right away. We invited everyone up to celebrate Christmas together, blending our families. My mom is seated next to Cade's parents. His grandparents are here, as are Ashlyn and her mother, Cash, Chloe, and Cameron.

Carter is standing up for Cade next to the fireplace, and Tory is walking down the aisle to music played by a string quartet. After she takes her place, the music changes and all heads turn to watch me descend the staircase.

I feel like I'm gliding on air as my beautiful organza gown floats down behind me. When I reach the bottom, Pike is there to join me, and we proceed down the aisle together.

"Dad always said you'd be a good man," Pike says to Cade when we arrive at the altar. "He was right. Take good care of her."

Cade shakes his hand and says, "I will."

I had hoped I could get through the ceremony without crying, but the gravity of this moment fills me with so much happiness and joy, the tears come. Not only am I marrying the love of my life, my brother is giving me away to his best friend. And, most importantly, he's happy about it.

Cade takes my hands in his. We promise to love each other forever, and then are pronounced husband and wife.

We toast, do a first dance, and then lead everyone to the dining room.

"Before we celebrate our union with an amazing meal," Cade says, "Palmer and I want to share something special with you. As you all now know, we dated secretly six years ago, and we want to share some of those moments with you. Cash, will you start the video?"

Cash dims the lights as photos of Cade and I together over the years flash across the screen.

"We were so happy then," I say, blissfully putting my head on his shoulder.

"We're even happier now," he replies, sliding his hand across my belly. "You know everyone is going to freak out over the last photo."

I smile at my husband and give him a kiss.

"Wait for it," Cade says, as the video comes to an end, revealing a photo of us kissing in front of the Christmas tree yesterday and holding out a sonogram photo.

"Is that what I think it is?" Cade's mother screeches.

My mother stands up and stares at the photo frozen on the screen, happy tears filling her eyes.

Both rush to give us hugs.

"When are you due?" they ask at the same time.

"July," Cade answers proudly, wrapping his arm around me as the rest of the room erupts in cheers.

# About the Author

Jillian is the *USA TODAY* bestselling author of fifteen novels. She writes fun romances with characters her readers fall in love with, from the boy next door in the *That Boy* trilogy to the daughter of a famous actress in *The Keatyn Chronicles* series. *The Keatyn Chronicles* is in the hands of over 600,000 readers and is a *USA TODAY* bestselling series. Her sexy contemporary romance, *Vegas Love*, is also a *USA TODAY* bestseller.

She's married to her college sweetheart, has two college-aged children who help with her business, two Labs named Cali and Camber, and lives in a small Florida beach town. When she's not working, she likes to decorate, paint, doodle, watch football and racing, drink good wine, and go to the beach.

Follow Jillian on her website.

**www.jilliandodd.net**

Made in the USA
Las Vegas, NV
08 February 2021

17508268R00155